A Note on the Author

JUSTIN CARTWRIGHT's novels include the Booker-shortlisted *In Every Face I Meet*, the Whitbread Novel Award-winner *Leading the Cheers*, the acclaimed *White Lightning*, shortlisted for the 2002 Whitbread Novel Award, *The Promise of Happiness*, selected for the Richard & Judy Book Club and winner of the 2005 Hawthornden Prize, *The Song Before It Is Sung*, *To Heaven By Water*, *Other People's Money*, winner of the Spears novel of the year and, most recently, the acclaimed *Lion Heart*. Justin Cartwright was born in South Africa and lives in London.

@justincartwrig1

UP AGAINST THE NIGHT

Justin Cartwright

BLOOMSBURY

LONDON · OXFORD · NEW YORK · NEW DELHI · SYDNEY

Bloomsbury Paperbacks
An imprint of Bloomsbury Publishing Plc

50 Bedford Square   1385 Broadway
London   New York
WC1B 3DP   NY 10018
UK   USA

www.bloomsbury.com

BLOOMSBURY and the Diana logo are trademarks of Bloomsbury Publishing Plc

First published in Great Britain 2015
This paperback edition first published in 2016

British Library Cataloguing-in-Publication Data
A catalogue record for this book is available from the British Library.

ISBN: HB: 978-1-4088-5822-6
TPB: 978-1-4088-5823-3
PB: 978-1-4088-5825-7
EPUB: 978-1-4088-5824-0

2 4 6 8 10 9 7 5 3 1

Typeset by Integra Software Services Pvt. Ltd
Printed and bound in Great Britain by CPI Group (UK) Ltd, Croydon CR0 4YY

To find out more about our authors and books visit www.bloomsbury.com.
Here you will find extracts, author interviews, details of forthcoming
events and the option to sign up for our newsletters.

For Jonathan Ball,
the indestructible

One [understanding] was of a society, and a section of society, that is violent, self-obsessed and contemptuous of the law. It was a lawlessness that represents a certain kind of South African impulse, not just an Afrikaner impulse

Mark Gevisser

We read landscapes, we interpret their forms, in the light of our own experience and memory, and that of our shared cultural memory

Robert Macfarlane

6 February 1838, Zululand

From a distance, the Reverend Francis Owen, his wife, their servant, Jane Williams, and a twelve-year-old boy, William Wood, watched, helpless and terrified, as a thousand Zulu warriors fell on seventy unarmed Boers and beat them with clubs. The dead and dying were dragged the eight hundred yards from the great kraal, *the* isigodlo, *of King Dingane of the Zulus, to KwaMatiwane, the place of execution, where those who were still alive were clubbed to death. The bodies were left for the hyenas and the vultures and the jackals. The leader of the Boers, Piet Retief, was the last to be killed. His thirteen-year-old son, Cornelis, was one of the dead. The warriors moved on to where they were camped to find the women, children and servants. The helpless women, children and servants were clubbed and stabbed to death, and their bodies, too, were dragged to KwaMatiwane.*

The hillock of KwaMatiwane ran with dark red blood. Venous blood. Rivulets of blood became streams, and the streams became rills. Further down the hill, the blood was finally reclaimed by the dry soil, leaving, for a while, only a damp trace, which faded fast.

I

My Australian grandfather came from Queensland to fight in the Boer War. In a recently opened cache of tobacco-tinged photographs I saw that I have inherited his looks. We are uncannily alike. He was a private in the Queensland Mounted Infantry and stayed behind after the Boer War ended in order to marry my grandmother. He died soon after the Second World War and before I was born. My mother, beautiful though she was, lived under a cloud of insecurity, the fear of desertion.

Like my grandfather I am tall, with a large head; my face is strong and deeply etched, with blue eyes that are often fixed on the horizon as though I am expecting a revelation.

Recently I have begun to feel that I am an impostor, not really English and never will be, although I have lived among the English happily and gratefully for many years. When I came to Oxford I intended to become English, because I did not want to be identified with the apartheid government. Now, in my onrushing middle years, the notion of home occupies me as if I must finally decide who I am, although in reality there is no urgency to make a decision; certainly nobody is waiting eagerly for my pronouncement.

On my mother's side of the family, I am directly descended from Piet Retief, the Boer leader, famous for having been murdered, along with all his followers, by Dingane, King of the Zulus, in

1838. Retief and his followers saw themselves as departing the Cape Colony in a biblical exodus. The oppressors were, in my ancestor's understanding, the British of the Cape Colony, who had recently freed the slaves. Inadequate compensation for the freeing of his slaves was one of Piet Retief's main complaints. Another was the unruliness of the brown and black people that followed British rule.

Most of my life I have been reluctant to be associated with my ancestor; I believe that there is something rotten at the heart of the Retief story, at odds with the myths of heroism and sacrifice.

Recently, I have been researching Piet Retief's life and I see that exaggeration was a characteristic of the family who were major optimists, a quality they combined with wide-reaching incompetence, so that most of their many enterprises failed. Even the most famous Retief – Piet – demonstrated an unfounded and fatal confidence, perhaps a certain contempt, when he agreed, in February 1838, to enter the royal *kraal* of Dingane without weapons.

I dream about my daughter, Lucinda, as she was before she became a drug addict. I dream of the mountain. I dream of the sea crashing on the beach. I dream of water trickling along dry furrows. I dream of my Auntie Marie's tin-roofed farmhouse in the dreary flatlands. I dream of unhurried Afrikander cattle. I dream of snakes. I dream of near drowning; in this dream I am powerless as I try to swim back to the beach. In the implacable workings of dreams, the harder I swim, the further out the current takes me. I am being pulled out to sea. I am panicking. I know that the secret is to allow yourself to be carried out with the riptide, even to swim with the riptide, because all riptides lose power and you can then swim back

4

from another direction. Easy to say: in my dream I am swallowing water, losing the battle, exhausted. These dreams don't have a hierarchy of importance; they have no logic; they are disturbingly random as though my turbulent brain is trying, without success, to find something solid on which it can alight.

Now I am lying, barely half awake, in my house in Notting Hill. When I finally wake and get out of bed, I feel clammy, as if I have slept wrapped in a caul.

Dreams have no useful meaning, but I believe that they feed on anxieties: my ex-wife pays lawyers to send me vile letters and, mad though they are, they disturb my nights and make sleep impossible. These letters are often delivered by anonymous couriers on motorbikes or by anonymous drivers of white vans. Last night, after one of these deliveries crashed through the letterbox, I could not go back to sleep for two hours or more and as I lay there I thought of Larkin's poem, 'Aubade':

Waking at four to soundless dark, I stare.
In time the curtain edges will grow light.
Till then I see what's really always there:
Unresting death, a whole day nearer now,
Making all thought impossible but how
And where and when I shall myself die.

My ex-wife is on a mission to destroy me; she succeeds in unsettling me with her crazy demands and wild accusations. I dread them. After all these years I still cannot understand why she is so vindictive and nor do I know what it is she really wants; after all it was she who claimed to have fallen in love. She announced it confidently to me as if she were the beneficiary of a Papal bull. She is a Catholic and she gave the impression that her liaison had been sanctioned in conclave by a quorum of cardinals, all of them keen to cite me for my behaviour. The person my ex-wife chose to marry was my best man at our wedding, Roddy Squires, baptised Rodney. Roddy was once described to me as pointlessly and unconvincingly good-looking; there is something tragic about him with his easily provoked laugh, so loud it can cut through a crowded pub in Belgravia. His brief acting career is over. He is always on the verge of the solution to his financial problems; he is promised acting roles in Canada or a job setting up a lodge in the Seychelles or a lecture voyage on a liner, but nothing ever works out. He has admirers among the more desperate women in his circle. They see something romantic about him until they discover that his blond, vigorous hair and his confident donkey bray hide anxiety and confusion. Roddy and Georgina never made it to the altar: the infatuation lasted only a few months. Georgina's ever-unstable whims are not based on rationality but on the higher posturing. And Roddy was a triumph of appearance over reality.

Last night, as I often do, I thought of going with my lover, Nellie, as far away from Georgina as I could. This may be one of the reasons I am thinking about the notion of home, and what it means. A refuge is one interpretation.

When I was fully awake this morning, I made a double espresso. I felt calmed as soon as I took the first gulp, fortified by the knowledge that I would soon be going with Nellie to my house on the sea near Cape Town. Nellie has a soothing effect on me because she is gentle and calm. She has gone ahead to our house in the

New Forest. I adore Nellie. After many years, I have understood that love is not an end in itself, but a process of learning to know another fully. It is strange how a truth is often clothed in banality. Much of what I know has come to me as a gift from books. I have relied heavily on books in order to understand the world.

2

The Adventures of Pinocchio. My aunt pronounced it Pea-noak-ee-o, and so did I until I arrived in England more than thirty years ago. She would read to me in the living room – *sitkamer* in Afrikaans – on the farm, which was about a hundred miles south-west of Johannesburg. The farm was called Welgelegen, which means well-situated, although there were no obvious topographical features to justify this description; Welgelegen sat passively in miles of flat land, stranded.

My aunt had no electricity; the generator had died years ago and she read to me by candle and lantern light. In my mind this twilight world was associated with reading; I thought it was essential to full concentration, like the manipulation of light for emotional effect in a theatre or in a movie. The candles and the lamps made a gentle noise, different for each, but working in harmony. The lamps whooshed and sometimes whined like spirits in the wainscot and the candles fluttered, sputtering once in a while, and in this way prefiguring the death of the moths. Pursuing their destiny, which is to reach the light, moths immolated themselves doing just that. As their bodies exploded in the candle flame, there was a distinctly liquid *pop*. The wings burned fast, like very fine mulberry rice paper.

In the way that young children create a hierarchy of affection, I liked moths; I saw them as benign and fragile, clumsily naïve, certainly not equipped for the age of the candle. In those days animals and insects were rated, even by adults, according to their likeability. Crocodiles, which we had never actually seen, ranked lowest. A boy of nine from my school, Lionel Pargeter, was taken by a crocodile while fishing at St Lucia Bay. There was no definitive proof that Pargeter had been snatched by a crocodile – no eye-witness – but there were crocodile prints everywhere, which were uncannily like the dinosaur prints in an old book, *The Lost World*, about a dinosaur. Lionel Pargeter had vanished. His fishing rod was lying on the muddy bank.

Back at school in Cape Town, his bed was next to mine in Tommy Gentles House, which was named after a famous, and very small, rugby scrumhalf. An old boy of the school. The bed was not used for a term as a mark of respect. For those ten weeks I slept uneasily close to Lionel Pargeter's imago. His parents never recovered fully. They endowed a scholarship in his name, to demonstrate that something good could arise from the worst tragedy. Supercilious little shits that we were, we called it the 'croc scholarship'.

In Johannesburg we had a swimming pool, and a large, American, Dodge – ten years old, admittedly, but stately and running on Fluid Drive. I boasted to my friends that we had this Fluid Drive as though it was some sort of magic potion. In truth I had no idea what it was, but I thought it had a glamorous, seductive, ring to it; I was always keen to make an impression. And maybe this, too, is my Retief inheritance.

I was never told why, from the age of six, I was sent every year to stay with my aunt – my *tannie* – Marie for a month. Tannie

Marie spoke English fluently with a strong Afrikaans accent. In fact she was not my aunt, but my mother's; she was one of those people destined for *tannie*-dom whether she wanted it or not. *Tannie*-dom at that time was a respected condition but not one that made allowances for hope. A *tannie* had no hope of a glamorous life, a second marriage, nor of anything beyond domestic duties. For all I know, nothing has changed out there on the flatlands.

My Tannie Marie had once been a teacher at the English medium school in Potchefstroom but she made an unfortunate marriage to a travelling salesman from Liverpool. If the photographs do not lie, he was astonishingly good-looking, and his hair shone with Uppercut Pomade, but he was also a compulsive philanderer and perhaps even a conman. He was arrested in 1944 and died some years after the Second World War.

When I was sent as an emissary from the more sophisticated world of Johannesburg, Tannie Marie was living in the middle of nowhere in the old family farmhouse, with its fading red tin roof and its long verandahs, which allowed her to face west in the morning and east in the afternoon, in this way avoiding the sun. The view from the house was not inspiring but the house itself had a timeless and comforting style. There were spiny cacti in large jam tins dotted around the *stoep*; some of these cacti only flowered every second year. Fly screens protected the doors. Occasionally Tannie Marie went out to look at the vegetable garden or the hens and I would go with her. The hens were innocent creatures, resigned and domestic. I would feed them crushed maize off my hand. The pecking action felt like being lightly tattooed. Once, the rooster became puffed up and angry for no obvious reason and pecked me viciously, drawing blood from my thumb. My aunt said that the male of the species always caused trouble. I wonder now if that wasn't a general observation about the world she lived in.

Not far from the house, beyond a tumble-down rockery, which looked something like a palaeolithic burial site, there was a moribund cemetery of apricot trees, twisted, dry and neglected, surrounded by a wall of large, deep red rocks – dried blood in colour (the colour of many paintings by Mark Rothko) – where lizards lay, sunning themselves. Although most of the apricots were pockmarked, my aunt could collect enough usable fruit to make her famous *appelkoos konfyt* – apricot jam. The skin of apricots sent a current up my arm and into my teeth; the effect was unbearable, worse even than fingernails on a blackboard.

Whenever my aunt ventured off the *stoep*, she wore a large hat to keep her complexion intact. Men thrived in the sun and welcomed the teak colour it produced – although two of the cousins who were suspiciously brown avoided sunshine. It was said that there was a touch of the tar-brush in the family; at that time I had no idea what it meant.

Women of my aunt's generation stayed out of the sun; it was considered unladylike, although back in the Sodom and Gomorrah that was Johannesburg, my mother loved the sun and wore short panelled skirts on the tennis court and Jantzen swimsuits at the pool – *Just Wear a Smile and a Jantzen!* was the slogan. That is how I remember her, as an advertisement. My mother would stand elegantly on the coir mat of the diving board, before diving neatly, arms outstretched, toes forever pointed. Our pool was heavily chlorinated and the water turned my hair green by the end of the summer holiday.

I think now that my mother saw herself as belonging to a bigger world than the one she sprang from. I came to hear much later that she was cheerfully promiscuous before marriage and perhaps after. An old friend of hers, who I met in Johannesburg on a business trip, gave me this unsolicited information. He appeared to have mislaid the edit button, something that is common among the very old: they think that because there are no consequences for them, anything is acceptable. Or maybe they are losing their marbles.

My father explained that my mother sent me away to the farm so that she could spend time in the Karoo where the bone-dry air was said to be good for her illness; perhaps she was preparing me for a life without her. In fact I learned – again, many years later – that the visits to the Karoo and its healing properties were my mother's cover for visiting her lover, a man with a business that employed huge machines to dig out irrigation dams for farmers; he had become wealthy because dams were always needed to catch the infrequent rains. Among the local farmers the question of rain and its imminence came a close second to rugby as a topic of conversation. Irrigation, I learned, was a very important consideration too, probably almost as important as religion. It turned out that this lover paid my fees to the Episcopal College, in Cape Town, where I was sent at the age of eight.

Tannie Marie seemed to be marooned at Welgelegen. She had hardly any money and no obvious options other than to sit it out at the centre of this moribund farm, which had a mostly symbolic existence, a negligible substance, in the rackety life of the Retiefs. The farm was one of those places that contrive to leach out all spontaneity and joy. It was understood in those parts that possession of a farm conferred prestige on the owners, licensing the men in the family to think of themselves as landed gentry down at the Railway Tavern where they drank their Lion Lager. To my young eyes, the farm seemed to be run-down. The farm gates, necessary in sheep and cattle country, were no more than sections of barbed wire braced at one end by a not-too-straight stick which was attached with loops of wire to a more substantial post, made from the branches of the camel thorn tree. Often the black children would rush out as a car appeared, to open and close the gate in the hope of being given a cent or two. Opening the gate wasn't easy; sometimes two or three of these scrawny little children were required to wrestle the gate free of the post. In winter the children had streams of mucus flowing glacially from their noses, like melting candles. They lived in mud-brick huts with corrugated-iron roofs held in place by rocks and sometimes by pumpkins.

Looking back, I realise that the farm practised a form of slavery; as far as I can remember, the only form of payment was maize-meal, a mud house, a ration of milk from the cows, after the rich cream had been separated, and a small plot for each family to keep a few sheep and grow some maize of their own. There was nowhere these black workers could go without the consent of their white farmer bosses. When they ventured into town, the police waited to see the passes provided by the farmer; without the farmer's permission they could be thrown into jail and fined. They had no money, but sometimes more generous farmers would pay the fine when they were arrested.

To my mind these farm workers – mostly Tswana or Sotho – were very resourceful: they played a game that involved indentations in the sand, with stones or seeds as counters, a version of *mancala*. In Africa this game is widely played, sometimes on pieces of wood that have been intricately carved and decorated. The children made little wire-frame cars to push around the farm; they ran behind, using a long steering wheel to guide the car. They were also expert in making catapults and they showed me how to make them, with a branched stick, some inner tubes, and a patch of leather from the shoemaker in town. With the catapult I tried to kill mouse birds in the apricot trees. The children also showed me how to find ant lions; I spent hours feeding ants to them and in the process I became intimate with the baked and exhausted earth. Ant lions are vicious little creatures, like miniature crabs. They dig a funnel-shaped hole, and throw up very fine sand, so that when an ant wanders innocently down into one of these holes it cannot get out. At the moment it slips back into the vortex of the funnel, the ant lion seizes it with its pincers and drags it under the sand. The pincers contain a toxin.

My Tannie Marie was a gentle person, perhaps even a timid person, and sad stories in books caused her to weep. I also cried easily as a child, probably because of the anxieties of my beloved mother's absences and early death, and this tendency has followed me into adulthood. Even now as I remember the room and my aunt sitting very close, reading *Pinocchio* to me – the moths committing discreet suicide – tears seep into my eyes. I think that Tannie Marie knew more about my mother and my grandmother than she let on. She had her own memories and disappointments to contend with, and her face, which was deeply creased, despite her regime of sun avoidance, would collapse into even deeper disarray. She would reach for the handkerchief she kept up her sleeve, snuffle once or twice, and dab her eyes. The skin of her arms hung down loosely, like the dewlaps of the cattle. She was enveloped in a slightly musky but not unpleasant micro-climate, scented with lavender.

I think that it was Tannie Marie's brothers and their harum-scarum sons who moved cattle in and out after they had bought them in the sales. There were always sales, some of them of house-hold furniture and ploughs and tractors and harrows, as farmers left the land. The cattle, long-horned Afrikanders, stood about morosely – big, glossy, humped animals, favoured by their name-sakes, the Afrikaner people. These cattle had a secondary role, as symbols of Afrikaner persistence and singularity. In their own way they were totems.

The cattle were fed teff – local hay – and dried lucerne to fatten them up before they were driven to the abattoir, in Afrikaans *die slaghuis*, literally the slaughterhouse. Afrikaans is a very direct language; maybe the original Dutch and Huguenots had difficulty describing their overwhelming surroundings, so they named rivers and farms and mountains without poetry and perhaps in too great a haste. For instance the local river was called Mooirivier, Beautiful River.

I have wondered if the drift to cruelty and violence was the effect of living in a harsh and unfamiliar land. Nelson Mandela once made this point: he said that the first Afrikaners were frightened by Africa and learned to hate black people out of fear. As memories of Holland and France faded, it may be that these Afrikaners became hardened in their fears of imminent danger, *die swartgevaar*, the black peril. Over the years, their names changed: Retief was originally a Huguenot name, Retif, from the banks of the lower Loire. The French was transliterated into Afrikaans, so that the pronunciation would remain the same.

It may have been her brothers and their sons who kept my aunt on the farm, to live uncertain of her purpose or her future, in the old tin-roofed house which faded from red to washed-out pink as the sun rose higher; every day before the cool winters arrived, she would sit on the *stoep* for her tea. She spoke Afrikaans to the women servants. These women were privileged; they were allowed to enter the house while the men had to wait outside the kitchen to be heard or to receive instructions. There was a threshold and they were never to cross it. I could see that these black people liked my aunt. She had an especially gentle way with the three women, who were known collectively as *meide*, maids, whatever their tasks. They were dressed at all times in aprons and *kappies* – little bonnets – which were worn and frayed but always clean. There was no money to go to Berman's General Supplies, the Jewish store in town, which my aunt described as an Aladdin's Cave. There in the profusion of iron pots and soap and buttons and brushes and buckets, Berman's General Supplies had bales of cloth for dressmaking, which my aunt liked to caress, but was never able to buy. The Jews had arrived after the Boer War. Everyone said they were good at business.

The younger maids walked with a slow sliding action, their bare feet dragging along the old Oregon pine and red-cement floors, so that I could hear them coming, making a noise like a gentle wave on a beach. I can hear it now. I am sixty years old.

At my house near Cape Town, close to the sea, I wake every day to the pounding of the waves. Sometimes it is wild, at others it is no more than a soothing whisper; from my bedroom I can judge the strength of the waves by the resonance carried on the south-easter. I have been entranced by the sea and its forces. If the weather was stormy, we sang a hymn in the school chapel for those in peril on the sea. I wondered how this plangent hymn was going to help as the waves flowed over the decks of fishing boats and the engines cut out. I have read that the Haida people of the western coastline of Canada regard the sea as more benign than the land. In their minds, the dangers and betrayals of the landlubber's life are far more treacherous and unpredictable than life on the ocean, which is subject to elemental rules.

Now that I look back across all those years, I wonder why Tannie Marie chose to read to me from *Pinocchio*. *Pinocchio* was written by Carlo Collodi in the 1880s and, in an old tradition of children's writing, it had a moral message: the message was that Pinocchio, if he was brave, truthful and unselfish, could become a real boy rather than a wooden puppet. Maybe Tannie Marie saw herself as my Geppetto, my creator. And in a way she was, because it was she who started me reading.

Outside, as she read to me, the sheep would be hanging their heads low, their blue-tinged tongues listlessly feeling out the dry paddocks – *camps* – for grass or sticking close to the wind pump with its lifeless sails. We called these pumps 'windmills' but they did no milling. When the wind blew it set the mechanism in motion; at first there was a harsh clanking and a reluctant crashing of gears before a trickle of cold, life-giving water appeared from a pipe that led directly into the tank, creating a minor turbulence. There was always a sense of relief when water was flowing again. Where the water overflowed, there was a small swamp, full of tadpoles and the occasional frog that was waiting for its moment to move on and escape the cattle egrets. I found it hard to believe that tadpoles turned into frogs and toads, and I was amazed when I saw the small froggy legs appearing on their sides.

In fact the dam was a round cement structure built on the ground, nothing more than a large tank. I was allowed to climb up a ladder to swim in an inflated inner tube, even though the water was destined for the house. In the afternoon the body of water would be warm and greenish.

Fascinated, I watched the water being directed into the furrows that irrigated the vegetable gardens before being directed, by pulling up one sluice gate and closing another, to the parched fields planted with maize and pumpkins. The first tongues of the water would roll down the furrows, gathering strength as the workers guided the water to the fields, the *lande*. I was watching a sort of parable, a demonstration in miniature of how to make the desert bloom. As the red soil was inundated, the water would itself become tinged with red. Sometimes frogs appeared from nowhere, rejoicing in their new domains, so I thought. Dragonflies would swoop over the inundated fields, snakes would flee, and white egrets would follow to see what had been made homeless and vulnerable. The land was thirsty; it sucked up the water greedily. As with the Mesopotamian marshes, which were drained and re-flooded, there was inescapably something biblical about the return of water to parched lands. In Africa, documentary film-makers often indicate the onset of the rainy season by filming the first trickles of water aggregating to become a flood.

There were other dams on the farm, hollowed out by tractors and small bulldozers and by gangs of black men with shovels; I saw the white contractors sitting under a lone pepper tree keeping an eye on the workers. Sometimes these workers were convicts, wearing shorts and a kind of shift; then a white man holding an old .303 rifle would keep watch on them. I saw one of these men beating a convict with a *sjambok*, a thick rhino-skin whip. When I told my aunt what I had seen, she said, *Yes, I know, it's terrible but what can we do? They are not our people. Onse mense*. Was she referring to the policemen or to the black people? I didn't ask.

Later my father, who was the editor of a campaigning newspaper in Johannesburg, revealed that, all over the Transvaal, warders in the Prison Service were renting out convicts very cheaply to their farmer friends. On a potato farm not far from Potchefstroom, my father's reporters discovered that five convicts on loan had been beaten to death by farmers. That's the way it was then. My father was accused of being a communist for this exposé. A dead dog was delivered to his office as a warning. He liked dogs, and his concern was for the dog rather than for himself.

I was full of eager anticipation when the windmills cranked up in response to the dry wind which arrived on a whim from nowhere and the water began to flow. I wondered where the water came from, and how it rested deep in the baked soil and how water diviners – usually drunks, I seem to remember – employed a cleft stick to find water. They would walk haphazardly about, following their dowsing rods, made from the branches of a tree with an affinity to water. I wanted to know why the water was so clear if it had soaked through the thick layer of cow dung that carpeted the *kraal*. It was from aquifers, deep down in rock, I was told. The black people used fresh cow dung to make the floors in their houses; it was spread flat with a plank from a fruit box, and allowed to dry hard and smooth. When dry it was odourless.

In many ways, I understood, the black people lived in their own, inscrutable, universe, one that existed almost unrecognised at the heart of the Afrikaner world. Nothing that black Africans did or said or believed was given a moment's consideration by the whites. It was as if what the black people wanted, or thought, or believed was of less than no consequence; it should all be forgotten, purged. It was also believed that black people were innately childish: all they wanted was food and a roof over their heads and a Christmas box or a bottle of cheap sherry. Even then I could see that these were self-serving beliefs. Strangely, some white farmers would go to the local *sangoma*, the witch doctor, for remedies. The *sangomas* could offer good luck, or remedies made from plants or cures for impotence.

I have more or less lost touch with my family in Potchefstroom, but I find that my days on the farm – how many days in all, I wonder – have left their mark on my mind, as though fifty years ago I was given a private viewing of another world.

One day my father appeared unannounced, bouncing down the farm road in his Dodge. Its suspension was designed for American highways. He said we were going home. My aunt packed my small case quickly and she cried as I left. She reached into the car to touch my face. I knew something catastrophic had happened. It was on the drive back to Johannesburg that my father told me my mother had died. It was difficult to take in.

'Daddy, you said she was getting better.'

'There were complications.'

'What are complications?'

'Things went wrong in the hospital. The doctors did their best. She fought bravely. Mummy said that you would always be her little man, and that she would watch over you from heaven.'

My father was an atheist but he was prepared to give up his principles to comfort me, and, out of bottomless desperation, I wanted to believe that my mother was in heaven, keeping an eye on me, her little *mannetjie*. I never saw my Tannie Marie again; I think now that my father decided we would have nothing more to do with my mother's family, as if they carried a kind of contagion, although he would never have said anything that harsh; he believed passionately in good manners. He wept in the car, and I was shocked to hear a grown man sobbing. I saw on his face, which was running with tears, just how serious the situation was, now that my beautiful mother was dead, and this disturbed me deeply. Through the tears my father could not see where he was going. We had to stop on the endless brown flatlands to gather ourselves. It was the first time my father had ever hugged me. He almost squeezed the life out of me in his demonstration of solidarity, so that I had to tap him on the shoulder with my free hand, like a wrestler conceding. In my mind's eye I seem to recall that we, entwined like figures by Rodin, were watched by two imperious blue cranes, the country's national bird – elegant and supercilious creatures, with a stiff, fastidious gait, as if they were

21

not wholly at ease with their surroundings and were treading cautiously.

Gradually my memories of my mother faded, although sometimes in the night I would be woken by an image of her diving into the green water. She was just thirty-three when she died.

3

Not so long ago, I was idling in my house in Notting Hill, when I saw an extraordinary clip on YouTube. Somewhere in the sea off the coast of South Africa, a man was swimming, wearing a head camera and carrying a spear gun. He was filming and describing what he was doing. Suddenly he became agitated. *Oo, vok my, Jissus nee, vok-of jou poes*. Loosely translated, he was saying, 'Oh, fuck me, Jesus, no, fuck off, you cunt.'

A great white shark, on an outing from the age of the dinosaur, was approaching him smoothly. In his distress, his Afrikaans probably seemed more apt than English, more effective against shark-attack anyway, because of its rich vocabulary of imperatives, honed over the centuries of instructing the brown and black peoples. When he broke the surface I recognised the voice: it was my much younger cousin, Jaco Retief, who I hadn't seen for nearly twenty years. He was now a man of about thirty-five, I calculated. As he swam, whooping hysterically, his voice was aerated by bubbles and his giant fins flailed away like windmills behind him.

But now the great white was coming back for a second look at Cousin Jaco and, to give him credit, Jaco dived and turned towards the shark – very bravely, I thought. The shark was as big as a house. Its face was inscrutable and cold, in the way that mass-murderers are always said to be emotionless. It was impossible to tell if the shark was hungry or just curious. Jaco held his flimsy spear gun with its puny harpoon, which was supposed to be propelled by a gas canister. This canister looked more like a can of beans than an offensive weapon, and now he pointed the spear gun at the shark as it came steadily closer with its smooth, suave face, that revealed two rows of huge teeth and what could have been mistaken for a smile.

Jaco was shouting at the oncoming horror: *Vok-of jou poes, vok-of!* But now the great white was approaching. Jaco turned towards the shark instinctively. He pointed his spear gun at the shark. The shark came steadily closer, suggesting that it might well be preparing to eat Jaco. When it was less than a metre away, Jaco prodded the shark with his spear gun, perhaps hoping to stab it in the eye. The spear gun barely dented the shark's skin, but – miraculously – it turned away and glided off into the murk. Jaco swam fast for a few minutes and climbed onto what was probably a paddle ski; I couldn't see clearly because he was creating a lot of turbulence. As he turned to see what it was up to, the shark surfaced very near the boat for a last assessment of Jaco's potential as a food-stuff, before turning and diving.

I remembered one of Carlo Collodi's stories about a giant shark swallowing first Geppetto and then Pinocchio; it looked as though my Cousin Jaco was about to suffer the same fate, although it seemed unlikely that Jaco would survive inside a shark, as Geppetto and Pinocchio had. It didn't occur to me immediately that the shark would have swallowed the head camera as well as Jaco. And of course then there would have been no YouTube record.

Jaco paddled frantically for the shore, and when he got there, still gibbering and shaking, he described to the camera what had happened: 'There I is looking for *kabeljou* or a steenbras and suddenly this fucking huge shark come towards me. I'm shitting myself. This is a monster, true's God, and I think I am fucked, for certain this huge fucker is going to eat me.'

In the middle of this piece to camera Jaco began to laugh. The laughter was not born of merriment, but hysteria. It was very disturbing. 'Every time what this fucker dives and I doesn't see him I'm thinking he's going to come up from under me at fifty kilometres an hour and chop me in two or come up to my paddle ski and then bite me and the boat in one hap. True's God, I am sure I am fucked.'

Now, bizarrely, he made a confession, weeping. He was seized by the idea that this was some sort of payback for neglecting his native religion, the Dutch Reformed Church.

I saw Jaco a few months later at the funeral for Tannie Marie, who had died aged ninety. The last time I had seen Cousin Jaco, he was on a school rugby tour of Britain and he came to visit me. He needed some money: he couldn't believe how fucking expensive London was. In return I went to watch him play rugby at Eton. To my mortification, he provoked a number of fights on the field. There was something about floppy Etonian hair and soft pale skin that enraged him, perhaps summoning in his mind images of the Boer War. After all, around nine hundred Boers, most of the women and children, had died in the British concentration camp at Potchesfstroom alone, not much more than a few miles from the farm. The following week Jaco was sent home after he punched a barman in Kent, where his team had just won a match 97–3. The three points were the product of a penalty awarded after Jaco stood on the opposing prop's head. He was on a mission of retribution.

Outside the church Jaco greeted me. His suit was too tight and his *boep* pushed vigorously against the lower buttons of his shirt. He gave me a card so that we could keep in touch. His face was pitted and he had lost his rugged, blond, Voortrekker appearance. The dominee preached in a strange, liturgical sing-song from within a brown suit roughly the colour of dried cow dung. I hadn't seen Tannie Marie for a long time: I wondered if *tannie* wasn't another Huguenot word in origin, from *tante*.

'I was shallow, very, very shallow behaved,' Jaco told me, revealing the depth of his new wisdom. 'A man shall have a close encounter with death so that he must understand what is really important for his children and his wife and such like.'

I can imagine that if you were convinced you were going to be eaten by a shark you might say more or less anything. In fact, Jaco had left his wife and children for a liaison with a woman he had met in Sun City. She was probably the 'such like'.

Jaco went on for five or ten minutes, sometimes exultantly born-again. He felt that he had betrayed the memory of our common ancestor, Piet Retief. I had the feeling that he wanted me to exonerate him. He was, I think, trying to make a complex biblical analogy between his encounter with a huge shark and Piet's encounter with one thousand Zulus. It was an analogy that, in my opinion, didn't quite work. Anyway, he proposed to give thanks publicly for his deliverance. It was all very unsettling and slightly mad. Soon after the funeral, Jaco achieved minor celebrity when

26

his video went viral. He gave inspirational talks about staring death in the face. (In this case a very large, inscrutable, face.) He gave interviews about sharks – he was, after all, an expert – and he forgot about his promise to make retribution to the Dutch Reformed Church; he also forgot his wife and two blond children, and even the woman from Sun City, a croupier, whose main job was to draw attention to her breasts rather than the cards, as drunk gamblers placed their bets.

Before he could don the promised hair shirt and recant publicly, Jaco was invited to go to California to talk about his shark encounter. He was introduced to Scientology and told he could learn about the superpowers that the Scientologists were promising him. They required him to hand over a lot of money, so that he could start his training as a pre-Clear, the first rung on the Scientologist ladder. He signed a contract binding him for a billion years. Jaco thought it was a deal: it seemed that with the help of superpowers he could live for ever or be reincarnated or, if he was diligent in his training, he could become a Thetan. As a Thetan he could float around the universe at will. He could even land on Mars if he felt the urge. 'At the very least,' to quote L. Ron Hubbard, 'this is the means that puts Scientologists into a new realm of ability enabling them to create the new world. It puts world-clearing within reach in the future.'

I wondered what 'world-clearing' means. It has unfortunate associations.

As a warm-up for acquiring Thetan powers, Cousin Jaco practised turning red traffic lights to green with the power of his mind alone, something which he had been told could be one of his skills if he trained hard enough. If he focused. With new insight, Jaco convinced himself that it was with his mind that he deterred the giant shark from eating him. His inspirational speeches now involved shark pacification, Dianetics, and the power Dianetics confers on the enlightened. But Jaco found the process of assessing his talents, which involved an electric lie-detector apparatus, the electro-psychometer – E-Meter for short – invented by L. Ron Hubbard himself – very disturbing. In the process of this 'auditing' he was expected to examine his previous lives and reveal his spiritual distress, as if escaping a huge shark in this life was not distress enough. He remembered an encounter in the sheep shed with a black woman when he was fourteen, but he couldn't bring himself to tell the auditor.

He spends some months at his studies and doing the tasks given to him. One day, when he is sent on a mission to deliver printing paper to the headquarters of Sea Org, he catches a glimpse of Tom Cruise. Cruise is playing tennis with his coach. Jaco is under instructions not to speak to anyone, and particularly not to Cruise.

4

In 1837, Piet Retief left the Cape Colony as the leader of a thousand ox wagons, heading north towards the Drakensberg Mountains, with a view to creating his new Canaan. Piet had sent out scouts to the Zulu King, Dingane: the lands to the east were reported to be very fertile and Dingane was agreeable to a meeting.

When Retief reached the Drakensberg Mountains, which bordered Zululand, most of the party stayed behind at a place they named Kerkenberg – Church Mountain – in acknowledgement of the huge standing rocks that suggested to them the nave of a church. This landscape below and the promise of boundless space it appeared to offer inspired his sixteen-year-old daughter, Debora Jacoba Johanna: on his fifty-seventh birthday she painted her father's name under a huge, overhanging rock. To this day it is visible, protected by a glass-fronted case, fixed there by people who believed that the Afrikaner heritage should be remembered.

Piet and a few of his men set out a few weeks later and rode east towards Dingane's *kraal*, uMgungundlovu, to meet the King. They wanted to ask Dingane to grant them land to settle. Instead of agreeing to the land grant, Dingane asked Piet to recover cattle stolen from him by the chief of the Tlokwa, Sekonyela. It was clearly a test: if Piet, using his miraculous guns and horses, returned his cattle, Dingane would sign the treaty the Boers had drawn up.

Piet and his men were astonished by the extent of the King's huts, the *isigodlo*. It was built according to the traditional layout of a Zulu royal *kraal*. In the middle of the *isigodlo* there was a huge empty space, the *ikhanda*, which was a parade ground. All along the perimeter of the *ikhanda* were the huts of the regiments, the barracks known as the *uhlangoti*.

As tradition specified, the royal complex was on a rise at the southern side of the complex facing the main entrance. The King, his wives and female attendants numbered five hundred, and the warriors at least another thousand. Every year at the ceremony of the first fruits, *umkhosi wokweshwama*, girls would parade and the king would choose new wives. In this way he was renewing the fertility of the land and the cattle and by choosing new wives the King became the symbol of this fertility.

The huts were beehive-shaped and each one was beautifully and intricately woven of thatching grass tied into the frame. The entrance of the huts was very low so that everyone had to stoop to enter. On each side of Dingane's hut, which was much bigger than the others, there were special quarters for his women and girls. The King's food and milk could only be handled by men, the *inzinceku*. It was a ritual of great importance, even something of a cult.

It occurs to me that these cattle played the same sort of totemic role as the Queen's horses. Years ago I took my daughter, Lucinda, to the Royal Mews behind Buckingham Palace. At that time Lucinda was having riding lessons. There was a distinct sense of cultic practice surrounding these gleaming and well-fed horses in their sumptuous stables, as if by keeping their coats glossy, their hooves oiled and shod, their manes cut evenly, their hay nets and fresh water abundantly available, a god was being propitiated.

Every morning the *inzinceku* milked the cows and carried the milk in gourds, their arms outstretched in front of them, to symbolise the avoidance of filth. Every morning these men poured milk straight into the King's mouth. They were privileged: where all other men had to crawl if they were approaching the King, the *inzinceku* could walk upright. And it was into this world – utterly alien, highly ritualised and casually brutal – that my ancestor stumbled, an innocent abroad.

Sekonyela had driven Dingane's cattle onto an inaccessible mountain; from the heights his men had rolled large rocks down on Dingane's warriors when they tried to recover the cattle. They were unable to dislodge these stubborn people. Guns were required. Piet agreed to take on the task. He returned to his camp near the Tugela River and soon set out again to find the stolen cattle. He was eager to acquire the fertile land that lay beneath him, a paradise of savannah, low, dense acacia woodland and wild rivers. The rivers tumbled down the escarpment in waterfalls which in turn fell into deep, turbulent pools, ringed by maidenhair ferns and shaded by huge yellow-wood trees in which vervet monkeys and baboons exchanged insults and threats. Lower down, the rivers levelled out, and here hippos carried on their noisy, crotchety lives and crocodiles were waiting in their limited but lethal fashion. All around there were antelope, elephants and lions. The lions and hyena often took cattle.

The Tlokwa were almost suicidal in their brave determination to resist and Retief's men shot and killed a number of them on the heights before they agreed to give up the stolen cattle, but not before a woman jumped with her children from the heights, shouting, 'I will not be killed by thunder, but I will kill myself.' Nobody knows whether she had met other white men and their guns.

On horseback, Retief and his men herded the errant cattle towards Dingane's country. At this season the landscape below was lush; Piet saw that livestock and crops would certainly thrive down there. He was sure that God had guided him to this promised land with a purpose. God had, in his omniscience, earmarked it for his favourite son.

A week later, on their tough, stocky, salted horses – immune to horse sickness – Piet and all his retinue were descending to uMgungundlovu with the richly patterned Nguni cattle stolen from Dingane. They proceeded slowly but remorselessly down the escarpment. The youngest boys – the *voorlopers* – herded the Nguni cattle and led the trek oxen, still attached to the wagons, and they held the oxen back to keep the wagons from running out of control. These boys were most probably Hottentots who had left the Cape with their parents who were in turn following their Boer masters. Who knows if they had a choice? The orders for the emigrating Boers specified that each family should provide ten Hottentots as well as oxen, foodstuffs, including rusks and dried meat, wagons, salt, kettles, household servants and a certain amount of money. This last demand may have been difficult for my ancestor, as he had recently been imprisoned for debt in the Cape Colony. The demand that each emigrating family should provide ten Hottentots suggests to me that they were still slaves, in Boer eyes anyway.

For the steep descent, the wheels on the wagons were locked by wooden brake-blocks, which began to smoke with the friction. The wood used was a soft wood, bush willow, for its grip and because it did not become as hot as other, hardwood, species, which quickly overheated, causing the iron rims of the ox-wagon wheels to expand and fall off. Wild peach wood was used to make the wheels. On their journey from the Cape, scores of wagon wheels were repaired and refitted.

Down below, some miles below, the thin smoke of the Zulu fires rose listlessly into the air. The Zulu *indunas* who had accompanied Retief to take back the cattle shouted the good news to their people below; their voices seemed to hang in the still air and from below other voices floated up to them. Many ran, overjoyed, to greet the return of the King's beautiful, sacred cattle and their restoration at the centre of Zulu life.

Behind the wagons, two huge black eagles – *ukhozi* – soared over the mountains, high above the promised land. Before he set out for the wilderness, 'New Eden' was the name Retief suggested for their enterprise.

I picture it all: a twelve-year-old boy, William Wood, is holding his grey pony's bridle as he observes the wagons coming closer. He is trying to count them. His horse is on edge; it has heard, long before William, the whinnies of other, unknown horses. William has an urgent message for the Boers, who are coming slowly but inexorably closer, streaming smoothly towards him. He is reminded of his mother's treacle cakes, which he misses. From a distance the wagons look like a river, but now individual wagons and oxen and horses are detaching themselves to become distinct entities, and the cracking of the whip, the bellows of the oxen and the shouts of the *voorlopers* waft down to William in the valley. He can even see the white bonnets of the women riding on the front of the wagons, perhaps a little nervous as they catch a glimpse of their New Eden.

When they finally reach the ford of the Nzolo River, which marks the way to the gently undulating lands surrounding the King's *kraal*, the Boers halt. One man rides towards William and waves his hat in his direction. William guesses that this is Piet Retief and raises his hat in return; he is not sure what else he can do. This man, who is on a sturdy bay horse, approaches William. He is striking, about fifty-five years old, with a black beard and blue eyes. On his head is a leather hat stained with mutton fat and dust. Over his shoulder is a leather pouch.

At first he speaks to the boy in Dutch:

'What are you doing here? What is your name? Are you the missionary's son? Do you speak Dutch?'

William says that he doesn't understand; he speaks English, but he says in mitigation that he also knows some Zulu.

The man on the horse asks the questions again in English and young Will tells the man on the horse his name and how he comes to be living here with the Reverend Francis Owen, a missionary. The man on the horse says that he is Piet Retief, and he is the leader of the emigrating Boers from the Cape Colony.

William asks him, 'What does "emigrating" mean, sir?'

'It means we have left our own country to live in another.'

'Why did you do that, sir?'

'Because, young William, we was discontented with the situation there.'

'Why were you discontented?'

'Our land, William, was taken over by the English.'

'I am English, sir.'

Retief laughs. He has a high, girlish laugh, all the more unexpected for rising out of a pitch-black beard.

'I won't hold you personally responsible, young William. Now tell me, where will I find the great King Dingane?'

William tells him that the King's *kraal* is just over the next hill, less than a mile away. Piet Retief asks him where he should make camp.

'Sir, if you make camp under the milk trees, beneath the Reverend Owen's hut, where I live, you will find water and grazing. Do not cross the river near his *kraal* before you have permission from the King.'

'First we must outspan the oxen so that they can drink and graze, and then we will go and see the great King. We have a present for him.'

'You have the King's cattle.'

'Yes, these cattle. We are bringing seven hundred head back to the King.'

Retief looks back to the wagons and gestures towards the cattle mottling the rich veld. They have spread out for hundreds of yards. Each animal's colouring is different; the Zulus recognise these patterns and have names for them; they call their markings *speckled eggs* or *pebbles* or *stones on a dry riverbed*; another is called *the shrike*, because its black-and-white marking reminds them of this bird, the fiscal shrike. Their descriptions are thousands of years old. The Zulus love their cattle. They also depend on them for meat and milk and hides; one hand, they say, washes the other. The *kraal*, the *sibaya*, is the centre of their lives. There are four cattle enclosures within the *sibaya*. The King and his people live in close proximity to their beloved cattle. The ceremonial royal cattle are black. No other cattle may mate with the royal cattle.

Retief has the gaze of a prophet; in the tradition of prophets his eyes see only what he wants to see, even things that are not visible. He appears to be looking at the horizon through his blue eyes. In his mind he perhaps sees his birthplace, the town of Wagenmakersvallei – Wagon Makers' Valley – resurrected here in this paradise. The English had renamed his home town Wellington, to honour the great hero.

'William.'

'Yes, sir?'

'You are a fine boy. You will meet my own son, Cornelis, who has thirteen years. He is here with me. You will be his friend.'

Retief points back towards the wagons, as if William needs to understand that his son is there, driving the cattle.

'Please call me Oom Piet – in the English language, Uncle Piet.'

King Dingane has also offered some young boys as companions for William. Oom Piet, his adoptive uncle, goes back to the wagons, his horse at a fast and comfortable triple, the favoured gait of the Boers.

William watches Retief riding off. He wishes he had been able to tell Retief what he had heard, that Dingane intended to murder him and all his men, women, children and servants. He has no opportunity to tell Mr Retief that Dingane sent a message, which said that he, the Reverend Francis Owen and his wife, and the other white woman, Jane Williams, a servant, would be safe. Despite this guarantee, William is frightened. In fact the guarantee of safety makes him particularly uneasy because it confirms that the Boers will not be spared. He wants to ride away on his horse, Snowy, to the coast and to his mother and father, but Dingane is mercurial and unpredictable and any show of weakness will almost certainly get him killed. If he tried to escape, the *impis* would follow him all the way to the coast if necessary. He must never give the impression to Dingane that he is frightened, because that will lead to certain death, as if by fearing death you are encouraging it.

He vaults onto Snowy, who is highly nervous and sweating heavily; they canter off in the direction of the mission. The mission is really no more than a large hut, although the Reverend Owen and his wife have made a garden and have given the place a kind of English cottage appearance. They have grown beans up a tepee-shaped arbour of sticks. They have tried to entice African honey-bees into a hive woven out of grass. For all that, there is an aura of neglect, as though their hearts have gone out of it. They have a cat, which intrigues the Zulus, who wonder what sort of medicine it is used for. The cat, Melbourne, travelled all the way from England with the Owens. It has learned how to kill snakes and so far has never been bitten. But it can only be a matter of time before a puff adder or a mamba gets him. Horses and cattle are often bitten when grazing and most of them die. This is an unforgiving land.

The Reverend Francis Owen and his wife have also been watching the cattle stream down from the escarpment, sticking close to their hut, and this probably gives them a false sense of security.

Owen's time in Zululand is more or less up; Dingane allowed him to preach once but he could not see the point of any of it and in particular he rejected the notion of sin and hell-fire. Who would sign up for that? This was Owen's one and only sermon.

William leaves Snowy with one of the servants and goes in to speak to Owen. The Reverend is talking to his wife. They look up, a little flustered, and smile unconvincingly, as people do when they are caught in private conversation. William sees that they are not suited to this life in the middle of nowhere.

'Ah, Will, did you talk with Mr Retief?'

'I did, sir. He has gone to make camp.'

'I saw them. There are at least eighty of them. Did you speak to their leader?'

'He was busy with the wagons and the stolen cattle, and only wanted to know where he should outspan.'

William knows that the Reverend Owen is deeply disturbed. These Boers – strange, brave people who have descended on them – are in terrible danger. And so is his small household. At the best of times, Dingane will kill anyone on a whim and if Owen tells the Boers that Dingane is planning to kill them, which he and William believe the King is intending, Dingane will know that it was he, Owen, who warned them and then he and his family will be swept up in the inevitable horror.

Half a mile from the huge royal *kraal* and facing the Reverend Owen's hut is the killing ground, KwaMatiwane. Hundreds, possibly thousands, of people who have crossed Dingane have been killed and eviscerated there. Random killing appals the Reverend Owen: he doesn't believe that the view from his home is suitable for a man of the cloth. The basics of Christianity have not taken hold here, and Owen wonders if they ever will. He is certainly not going to wait to find out. Since he was allowed to deliver his only sermon, Owen has not made a single convert. Now he is faced with an appallingly stark dilemma; if he warns the Boers, he and his household will almost certainly be killed; if he doesn't, the Boers will be killed. It is an ethical dilemma of the sort that professional philosophers like to wrestle with. Owen has searched his Bible for a precedent he can follow, and failed.

The question is stark: are the lives of his family more valuable than the lives of a hundred Boers and another hundred women, children and servants?

Owen is wracked.

Dingane receives Retief and invites him and his men to a ceremony in the *kraal* in a few days, to thank him for the return of the cattle. To celebrate, Retief's men gallop around on their horses firing their guns, perhaps showing off their power, unless it is nothing more than an ill-judged celebration of the return of the cattle. There is a delay; William hears whispers that Dingane is summoning his regiments from outlying villages. Two days later Retief and his men are asked to come to the *kraal*, and to leave their guns outside: it would not be appropriate to bear arms at a celebration in the presence of the King. The guns are stacked at the entrance of the *kraal*. The Boers are seated in the vast open space at the centre of the *kraal*, the *isibaya esikhulu*. There will be feasting and three traditional dances from Dingane's warriors. Dingane has seated Retief near him. The warriors are armed only with their short knobkerries, *isagilai*, which are something like a shillelagh and are used for ceremonial dances. The Boers look on, amused, but perhaps also with rising apprehension, as the Zulus stamp and leap and shout and advance ever closer to the Boers, so that the earth beneath them seems to shudder. Suddenly, on a signal from Dingane, more than a thousand warriors of the *amabutho*, the King's own regiments, stream into the *kraal*. Dingane stands up: '*Bulalani abathakathi*,' he calls out – 'Kill the wizards'. The warriors surround the seventy or eighty Boers, and club them with their sticks. One of these is Cornelis Retief, aged thirteen, who is now never to meet William Wood. Some of the Boers fight back with pocket knives, killing three or four Zulus, but they are soon overwhelmed. The warriors drag the Boers eight hundred yards from the royal *kraal* to KwaMatiwane, the place of killing, where the warriors finish off the living with their clubs. Zulu oral accounts relate that Retief was the last to be killed, so that he would be obliged to watch the agony of the massacre. I sometimes think of young Cornelis and I try to imagine how his father felt watching his son's death. I am related to Cornelis too.

Piet's heart is removed and taken to Dingane before being buried under the path leading to the *kraal*, a practice designed to keep the spirits of the dead at bay. The warriors jog some distance on towards the camp where the women, children and servants are waiting for the men to return; they are helpless as they hear the *impis* coming closer. The noise made by a Zulu *impi* running to battle is terrifying and said to be like the sound of waves on a beach. It is produced by the agitation of the porcupine-quill anklets all the warriors wear. The women, children and servants are killed. In all, one hundred and fifty Boers and their retainers die. The bodies of the women and children and servants too are dragged to the hill, KwaMatiwane, the place of killing, and left there for the lions and the hyenas and the smaller scavengers like jackals and bat-eared foxes and, in the daytime, vultures.

The Reverend Francis Owen and his household, including William Wood, watch in horror and fear. William has not told Owen that he has spoken to two of the Boers and warned them of the danger they are in. He has been unable to keep the secret. The men chose not to believe his warning; Dingane, they said, was a fine fellow.

Two years later William described the massacre in a written account. His father was on the expedition sent a few months after the massacre to punish Dingane. This expedition was routed and William's father was one of those killed. William records his father's death in a very matter-of-fact way. There is no eulogy and no expression of emotion. I wonder if he was traumatised. I think of my daughter and her troubled mind.

The vultures and the hyenas are busy on the killing fields for many days. At night the hyenas squabble over the bodies, whooping and screaming in their disturbed fashion. Lions also arrive to feast on the bodies. As dawn breaks, the male lions roar in turn, a sound that indicates that they are going to lie up in the shade, sated. Their roars broadcast a threat to interlopers, a threat which carries right up to the slopes of the high mountains. With daylight, the vultures – great hooded birds – circle once more before falling clumsily on the remains of the Boers, ripping and tearing at the flesh with their huge beaks, which are shaped like bill-hooks.

Soon after the massacre, Dingane spoke to Richard Hulley, a trader and translator: 'I see that every white man is an enemy to the black, and every black man an enemy to the white. They do not love each other and never will.'

In his last meeting with Owen, Dingane asked the very nervous missionary, 'Do you not see that I have done a good thing in killing my enemies in one stroke?'

Soon, Owen and his household are given permission to leave uMgungundlovu, although William waits some days, feigning nonchalance in case the King should think he is in an unseemly hurry to get away to Port Natal.

Owen admits in his diary that he went along with the King:

Two of the Boers paid me a visit this morning, and breakfasted, only two hours before they were called into another world. When I asked them what they thought of Dingaan, they said, 'He was good,' so unsuspicious were they of his intentions. To Dingaan's message this morning I sent as guarded a reply as I could; knowing that it would be both foolish and dangerous to accuse him, at such a season, of perfidy and cruelty. However, as his message to me was kind and well-intended, showing a regard to my feelings, as well as to my safety, I judged it prudent and proper to thank him for it.

Later Hulley wrote:

It appears clear from Mr Owen's evidence that, rightly or wrongly, Dingaan thought the Boers intended to kill him, and that he meant to anticipate their plot by killing them.

Owen wrote up his every day's happenings. But what does not appear in his diary is any guilt for dooming the Boers to be 'called to another world'.

It is clear to me that Dingane believed that the piece of paper he had signed two days before the massacre was a ruse to steal his land. Under Zulu custom, the land belongs for ever to God and not even a king has the right to give it to others. When I read that Dingane shouted to his waiting warriors, '*Bulalani abathakathi*' – 'Kill the wizards' – I wondered what, exactly, he meant. I remembered from my first – and only – year at Oxford that Wittgenstein said, 'Language sets everyone the same traps; it is an immense network of easily accessible wrong turnings.' And I discovered that the term '*abathakathi*' indicates not sorcerers or wizards in general, but those whose intentions are always malign. I have learned that there are terms in Zulu for black and white wizards, a concept similar to white and black witches in Europe. In fact I remembered a painting by Cranach the Elder that depicts witches on horseback. So Dingane's sight of galloping horsemen firing guns, led by Piet Retief, may have suggested frightening supernatural powers.

Retief – cloaked in righteousness, blessed by God, free of his creditors – had undoubtedly arrived in this land in order to take it. And despite the fact that he was still just about living on the cusp of prehistory, Dingane understood what was in store for his people. His conversation with Hulley confirms it, and the subsequent history of South Africa bears witness to the fact that whites seldom observed the treaties they had made.

In December Dingane sent his warriors against another group of trekkers, who were led by Andries Wilhelmus Jacobus Pretorius. Dingane's warriors attacked the circle of wagons on the banks of what came to be called Blood River. It is said that, without a single Boer being killed, three thousand Zulus died that day. The Boers saw it as a sign from God that they had his approval for their biblical journey into the wilderness. And I think it established the idea of necessary violence that the Boers adopted wherever they went.

On 29 January 1840, a combined force of disaffected warriors and followers of Mpande, Dingane's half-brother, along with English irregulars from the coast and Pretorius's Boers, defeated Dingane's warriors. In a rage, Dingane had his general, Ndlela ka Sompisi, executed. But soon after, the King was driven into the forests, and was assassinated at Hlatikulu. For the Boers, victory was complete, but I wonder at what cost to subsequent history.

The kingdom of Zululand still exists, but in reality it was finally crushed by the British in the Zulu Wars of 1879. Both sides suffered appalling casualties. Yet the allure of the Zulus as the warrior nation persists.

One of the most moving plays I have ever seen was the Zulu *Macbeth, Umabatha*, staged in Johannesburg. When the Zulu warriors bounded onto the huge stage, the audience began to cheer and ululate; it was clear that the actors and the audience understood with a passion that this was also the history of Zulu regicide and violence; Duncan was Dingane. At that time the Zulus were holding out against the first free elections and Johannesburg was tense. I was there as an official observer. There had been a huge explosion near the Town Hall, which killed nine people. I had the sense of being in a war zone, in part thrilling, in part terrifying. At the time it seemed to me to be one of those experiences which change you for ever.

5

Notting Hill has a raffish elegance. Bankers have long ago caused property prices to rise way beyond the means of the vast majority. Once it was run down, but now the gleaming stucco houses advertise wealth and entitlement. They are encased in so many coats of white paint that they look like huge chunks carved from an iceberg. I was lucky – I bought here cheaply more than twenty-five years ago. Once again property prices are in the news. London is obsessed with property prices. Are they too high? Is the bubble going to burst? An apartment was sold recently for £140 million. Earlier inhabitants think that Notting Hill has been ruined.

Winter has come. I am off to Cape Town where I was born. Every year as the northern winter arrives, I leave for my house on the sea. It takes ten minutes to walk from my front door to the Underground, past the old Coronet Cinema, where I spent hours out of the cold when I first came to London. Down here, on the Central Line, deep under London, maverick blasts of warm air reach us. I look at my fellow travellers and make a sort of assessment, as though I am mandated to make these judgements: are there more Chinese than usual? Are there many more Eastern Europeans? Are those men with the sticky-up haircuts hedge-fund boys heading for the City? Are these men in cheap tracksuits asylum seekers? Is this worried man, leafing backwards and forwards in a dog-eared book, perhaps looking desperately for inspiration, a novelist? I see no theme today: there is just resignation in dulled eyes. The passengers are subdued: *depression hangs over them as if they were Iceland*, to misquote. Beneath the skin around their noses and on their eyelids, I see a chafed redness emerging determinedly. It is like a pentimento, the earlier pigments fading, to expose what is underneath. Today the summer pigment is fading, to reveal the faces of winter.

A woman of about forty-five years old is holding a compact and using a brush on her eyelashes. She has to peer out of one eye as she works on the other; she cocks her head and moistens her mouth; unsatisfied, she touches up her lashes with a second, stronger, application of eyeshadow. Time and again she looks at herself in the mirror, improving her work. Now she is applying some glittery material, perhaps eyeshadow, to her brown smoky eyelids with a brush. I feel for her; she seems to be very anxious, as if she is going for a job interview. Or she may be trying to look young and alluring. In its small scale, it contains a tragedy. My ex-wife – how welcome the 'ex' is – would have said I was patronising, but I know that women have a more difficult path through life than men. Childbirth is profoundly important for women and it endows them with arcane knowledge, not accessible to men.

I admire the English and I believe I almost understand them. I have a few paintings, among them an Ivon Hitchens and a Paul Nash. I like to think that I haven't bought them for any reason other than because they speak to me of their Englishness. I have tried to surround myself with beauty, and sometimes I think that it is the only important thing that money has given me.

In South Africa my family had two numinous paintings by the Afrikaner painter, Hendrik Pierneef, which celebrated the Boers and their remote farms. These paintings contained a message for the Afrikaners of divine blessing in their search for a new Eden among the heathens. My father said the paintings were 'of their time'. In those days quite a lot of things were excused by this phrase.

The economy has improved, but people complain about the cost of living. When I arrived in London in 1982 I had nothing. Now I am fairly wealthy; I have the house in Notting Hill, a farmhouse in the New Forest, where I am the friend of New Forest ponies, deer and many types of bird; I know where to find the secret hiding places of chanterelles and parasol mushrooms. Also, I have the beach house a few miles south of Cape Town, a house that is inspired by Martha's Vineyard: it is pale blue and white with a broad, bleached deck overlooking the sea and a garden that tumbles down the hill.

I am going to pick up the Mercedes, which has been serviced, and then I will drive down to the New Forest to lock up for the winter before I fly to Cape Town where we will meet Lucinda, my daughter. Nellie, my lover, is coming too, possibly with her son, Bertil.

I emerge from the Underground at Marble Arch and I walk down Park Lane. According to the *London Mail* this is now the bridgehead for Romanian gypsies whose presence has been exercising the editor. According to her, Hyde Park will soon be a gypsy encampment, with barefoot urchins gathering unspeakable bits of meat from bins outside restaurants, to be boiled for hours on fires fuelled by chopping down the ancient oaks of Hyde Park at night – the oak, England's symbolic tree, for God's sake. Bulldogs, oak trees, bobbies, all on the way out as symbols, along with standard English. At the moment I can count just four people who could be Romanians, no doubt the advance party, the pathfinders, for the masses to come.

It is true of all great cities that they have many faces. Most of the time I love London immoderately, but when the afternoons darken and close, I feel a claustrophobic depression descending on me. Today the sky is clear and still, so still that Hyde Park is frozen in a landscape painting – a day, an hour, a moment preserved. The grasslands are coated in frost. I can see horses cantering reluctantly on the bridleway. I know horses. Livery horses move wearily because they are bored with the endless circuits; they live without the possibility of novelty. The English feel they have a special bond with horses; more upper-class women are killed falling off a horse than in any other causes, including road crashes and drug abuse. I love horses for their decency.

The Christmas lights on the trees and on the grand buildings of Park Lane are struggling to be seen, so clear and low and adamantine is the afternoon light. Anything is possible today, I think.

I speak to Nellie from the car. She is already there, busy in the house. She asks me if I am happy. She always asks me this question and it always warms me. There is ease and tranquillity between us, something I have not experienced before. I say yes, thanks to you, I am happy, even ecstatic, although at the moment my happiness has a persistent undertow of anxiety: my daughter has been discharged from rehab in California and is coming to Cape Town to stay with us. Her drug-taking, I am convinced, was a reaction to my break-up with my wife. Maybe all broken marriages cause cracks to open in the self-esteem, and even in the souls, of children. The pain my ex-wife and I caused our daughter will be on my conscience until the day I die.

Lucinda sided with me when Georgina and I separated. Together she and I weathered the onslaught of Georgina's lawyers. My wealth, Georgina will tell anyone who is prepared to listen – and some who are not – is her wealth. It is not true. Her story goes on to relate that, with the help of crooked lawyers, I was able to prise open the family vaults. The truth is that I knew that her family had a fancy tax-avoidance scheme in the Isle of Man and I kept this to myself until I had to play my trump card.

Georgina raged about how I had spent her money; she had forgotten that it was she who bought large and decrepit houses in Notting Hill and turned them into lavish boutique hotels which failed and she forgot that it was she who set up doomed businesses which were intended to help the coffee growers of Nicaragua or to finance remote Indian communities in making saris or to support a cooperative in Venezuela which empowered women or to bring fresh water to impoverished villages in Zimbabwe – and many other causes.

She loved her philanthropic work because it allowed her to mix with pop stars and models and designers and it allowed her to ignore the administration of the finances as she engaged in this high-altitude life. She saw no irony in rubbing up against rich pop stars, who are the visionaries of our era. At the same time she never cared for writers, unless they were huge best-sellers, as if sales were the only validation of a writer. She lives in a visual world.

All her enterprises ended in theft, corruption and lawsuits. Many millions of her father's legacy were lost. I tried to warn her and she interpreted these warnings as jealousy or a desire to control her. She said that men like me were incapable of giving women respect and space. She grew very still when I gave her advice, lifting her head and looking away as though she was hoping to see something more congenial and pleasant to rest her gaze on. I grew to loathe her, and this hatred affected Lucinda.

One day Georgina declared that she was in love with a friend of my best man, and she demanded a divorce. I didn't contest it; as a matter of fact I was delighted. The judge was something of a Leveller; he didn't warm to Georgina's family and its sense of entitlement, nor to the blustering and expensive QC who was drafted in at the last minute to oppose the settlement. A small, almost visible, cloud of self-esteem circled him, like one of those planets that are loosely wrapped in vapour and trailed by clouds of red dust. Or perhaps like an egg poaching in a little whirlpool of attendant egg white. But when I mentioned the family's Isle of Man scheme, the QC quickly advised a settlement. Georgina described it to her friends as blackmail and they were quick to pass her opinion on to me. This all happened five years ago.

As the result of this warfare, Lucinda had started to take drugs at her school and she quickly descended into drug hell. It happened very quickly, too quickly for me to understand or to recognise. Later she told me that drugs were available everywhere; in London, she said, if you were on heroin you were able to buy the stuff absolutely anywhere and you could find a dealer even in the smallest rural village. As a user you are able to spot dealers without difficulty; she said that, like the proximity of rats in London, you are never more than a few yards from a dealer. The dealers will unerringly recognise the addicts.

Her problems have tormented me, because I know that Georgina and I were blinded by a bitterness that ran wildly out of control and destroyed our beloved child. Incongruously, I think of the African savannah when a sudden lightning strike ignites the dry grass. I seem to have acquired my own, African, set of metaphors. In some inexplicable way I believe that the African landscape exists deep within me, imprinted indelibly many years ago. My reveries often involve Africa. For instance, I remember my Tannie Marie's farm and the huge raindrops falling on the tin roof and I remember the hail which followed, as big as golf balls, bouncing on the farm road and creating an arctic landscape which soon melted; I remember the forlorn bleating of the sheep lined up to be dunked after shearing in a plunge dip full of cloudy, pungent chemicals. And I remember vividly the black people who worked on the farm and who gave me mealie porridge from their cast-iron pots. I recalled how they rolled the porridge into a fat cigar shape and handed it to me with a delicately cupped hand; the skin of the palms of their hands was lined, strangely pale, and their eyes often had a yellow cast. Sometimes they gave me the porridge soaked in fermented milk, *amasi*, which Tannie Marie called *maas*. I think there must surely be some connection. I remember when Nestlé promoted an African drink on Springbok Radio: *Introducing new Nestlé Make-it-Yourself Maas. Made from real milk to give you all the taste of traditional creamy home-made maas.* We pronounced 'Nestlé' as 'Nessles'.

The black people, who had so little, were invariably kind to me; they were a little curious and perhaps a little concerned about a small white boy wandering around this derelict place.

All these things, all these whispered messages, are becoming more important to me, as though I am hearing a lost language or a distantly remembered tune.

6

When I last saw her in California, nearly a year ago, Lucinda looked a lot better than she had been. At her worst, her face was strangely clotted, her features mysteriously rearranged – like ice floes that had jostled each other – and her eyes had become small and defensive as though she was wary of some violence or maybe just some gratuitous unkindness. I wonder if I am not imagining this. Is it possible for eyes to become smaller? After twenty months of expensive treatments at a clinic overlooking a bay in Marin County, north of San Francisco, which was apparently made restful by the sound of the nearby waves, she has recovered, although she has a tendency to talk about herself and her karma relentlessly. She may still believe in positive energy; she has gathered it wholesale in California. Dr Hirsch, her psych and mentor, wrote to me, with her permission, to pronounce her clean.

Lucinda has never been to the beach house but I am hoping she will love it. She will be able to hear the waves falling on the beach and maybe that will keep her calm. It is encouraging that she has agreed to come at all; perhaps she has shaken off her torpor. As a child she was always cheerful and eager so the decline into drugs was terrifying, as if another person was inhabiting her delicate and familiar body without permission, a form of kidnap.

I find the crashing of the waves on the beach below my house uplifting, as though they are designed particularly to speak to me, to confirm that I live somewhere wild and elemental and dangerous. Larcenous baboons come to visit us occasionally. Once we found stranded whales on the beach, and three years ago a seventeen-year-old boy was thrown off his surfboard and driven by a huge wave into some enormous, egg-shaped rocks where his arm became wedged high up in a cleft. As the tide came in we tried desperately to save him. It was a nightmare, with all the helplessness that entails: each incoming wave rushed over him more strongly. He would soon be underwater. Three of us swam out to the rocks and for a few long minutes I had his arm in my hands, trying to pull it free, but as the waves grew more insistent his arm was wedged more tightly and I was dragged away by the giant swell. Less than half an hour later he was completely submerged and he drowned in full sight. It was appalling.

We commissioned a bench, made of driftwood, in his memory, all of us understanding that he had done something worthwhile in taking on the giant waves. We shared a sense that he had given up his life for others, by voluntarily taking on the unforgiving sea, perhaps trying to subdue it on our behalf.

We had a bronze plaque made for the bench:

Nothing of him that doth fade/ But doth suffer a sea change/ Into something rich and strange.

I suggested these lines from *The Tempest*, lines that also commemorate Shelley in the Protestant Church of Rome. Familiar lines, but comforting in their promise of continuity.

Now Georgina is forty-six. She is trying to have another baby with the unscrupulous encouragement of an *in vitro* specialist. She believes she can buy anything and, up to a point, she is right. The donor is her new partner. I have met this man: he is called Ranulph, a friend of the man she ran off with the first time. The image of Ranulph providing sperm for my ex-wife's purposes makes me feel queasy; I see it as an act of aggression directed to me and to Lucinda. I can only guess how Lucinda will react to this latest betrayal.

I was a difficult husband, but it was because I hardly ever agreed with Georgina on any issue of taste or judgement. I would quibble about all sorts of things, not because I believed in what I was saying, but as a form of hostility. I had reached rock bottom. I was losing my humanity.

Our house was increasingly a source of distress to me: it looked like an advertisement for one of Georgina's doomed boutique hotels, strangled by swags and plumped by garish cushions; the knick-knacks twinkled at night and the whole place had the feeling of a seraglio painted by John Frederick Lewis. I felt endangered as I sat on a sofa, as though a giant clam was about to swallow me. Georgina believes fervently in the supreme importance of design; for her it is a fundamentalist faith.

The things that were important to me, like books, were redundant to her – old school – as if there were exciting new currents of energy dashing about that I was not tuned in to. I remember something I read a few months before: 'I have beliefs, but I don't believe in them.' I take this to mean that there are conventional beliefs – serviceable, everyday beliefs – which are handy but really no more than placebos. And then there are deeper questions about the unknowable mysteries, like death, the importance of great art, the impossibility of knowing another's mind and the nature of culture.

Georgina is still keeping tabs on me and she pays close attention to any potentially lasting relationships. For instance my love affair with Nellie Erikson, who is Swedish and forty-one years old, nearly twenty younger than me. I met her at a dinner party given by my friend, Zoe. She told me later that she had been match-making: it was obvious that I needed a wife. Women do this so as to patch up the cracks in the human fabric. Nellie and her husband, Lars, were in the throes of a divorce because of his drinking. She told me about Lars and I told her about Georgina and I fell in love with her that evening. We were both adrift and clung together.

'Thank God for you,' I said to Zoe one day. 'Nellie has changed my life.'

'I was worried about you. Now you look happy again.'

'Was it that obvious?'

'Yes. Sorry to say so, but yes, it was. In fact you looked miserable. You weren't shaving properly either. That's a sign. Frank, there aren't many good men about, but you are one of them. Georgina was horrendous. We all knew. We all felt sorry for you.'

'Thank you. Thank you, Zoe.'

Even so I felt a little affronted that she and her friends should feel free to pass judgement in this way. Nothing in a marriage is what it seems to be.

Georgina sends emails filling me in on Nellie's past; at various times she has said that Nellie is an obsessive and that she is the daughter of a Swedish fraudster. Also, according to Georgina, Nellie is one of those women approaching middle age who spend their whole lives in spas and gyms because they are insecure. But her letters are mostly reserved for more serious charges against me; I really belong in jail for stealing her money. Her worst charge is that I drove our daughter away. This accusation upset me for days. I had thoughts of killing her. I called, breaking my rule of never starting a conversation with her.

'Georgina, look, can I ask you not to make wild accusations about what I did to Lucinda?'

'Oh dear, are we upset? What can I say? You threw her out. That is the fact. You did it to get at me.'

'Oh Jesus, this is borderline certifiable. You had no relationship with her, she loathes you, you ran off with that fruitcake, and all her life you were always putting Lucinda down.'

'You threw her clothes out on the street.'

'The psychiatrist said we had to get her out of the house so that she could try to work out her problems herself. He said it was the only way forward. You know what he said. We discussed it many times.'

'You just wanted to get rid of her for selfish reasons. You hid behind the psychiatrist. Out of sight, out of mind. That was your policy.'

I felt as though a stroke was coming on. I didn't speak to her for months.

She still calls me, ostensibly to talk about Lucinda, which of course I can't refuse, but she quickly returns to the subject of Nellie: 'What do you think she is looking for with all that yoga stuff? Mental stability?'

She is also dangerously thin, apparently, verging on the anorexic. I wonder why Georgina, who tells people she hates me, is so interested in my life. And I wonder where Georgina gets her information. Maybe she manufactures it to order. While accusing Nellie of these crimes, she is proposing to have a baby via a test tube, with Ranulph, who is a failed estate agent. And this is a baby whose only purpose will be to increase Georgina's self-esteem, which is already, if you ask me, dangerously inflated.

The New Forest in winter is faceted with dew so that the gorse and the grass sparkle in the late, low sunshine. The ponies are lively; at this time of year a few select stallions, highly sexed little boulevardiers, are released onto the forest for a short time, to launch a kind of horsey bacchanalia which will improve equine diversity.

As I pull up in front of the house, Nellie comes out. She is holding a huge bunch of coppery hydrangeas and wine-dark sedum. Her blonde hair is tied back loosely. My dark thoughts fade away. She always looks happy to see me, and my heart lurches in response – I am conscious of the overburdened heart, responsible both for our blood supply and our emotions. Her chin is large and her blue eyes are some way apart, an almost feral arrangement which I have learned is typical of Swedes. She looks in this regard like Agnetha of Abba, beautiful in an elusive way. When she kisses me I feel blessed. As her softly pliant mouth meets my rough cheek I am keenly aware that we are made of different materials. I am built for another sort of life, a life long gone.

'Hold me: you are like a bear.'

'A bear?'

'Yes, and you see many things.'

'What things?'

'All sorts of things. You are unravelling the secrets around you. You are always on a journey.'

My arms are around her slender, responsive body; I am strangely flattered by what she said even though I don't know what she means. I take it as a compliment.

The flowers are squeezed between us for a moment. There is something so serene and reasonable about Nellie that, after all the years of reproach and criticism and argument and silent rage, I am at last calm. Her body has a natural talent for fitting itself very closely to mine, hugging the contours; I told her that she was like a gecko on a wall, but she didn't know what a gecko was. Apparently they don't exist in Sweden.

I unpack the car and join her in the house; she is arranging the flowers now in a blue-tinged Kosta Boda vase; a swirling blue infiltrates the clear glass in streams, like offshoots of the Northern Lights. Nellie goes in for the simple and the seasonal. Georgina ordered single hothouse stems of tall red amaryllis in bud and she arranged them in glass bowls. Sometimes she cut off the stems and launched the amaryllis heads in huge shallow dishes – an oriental touch – dotted with small candles floating on the surface. My Tannie Marie had just a few prickly pear flowers in jam tins and, deep down, I still see perfect, over-bred and cosseted flowers as pretension, a sort of indulgence.

Nellie has lit a fire in the Swedish stove, and the scent of wood smoke fills the house. She has brought herring and yellow peas for soup and gravadlax and meatballs.

'Thanks for all this.'

'What do you mean?' she asks.

'You know Nellie, you know. I am so completely happy just to be with you. I long to see you when we are not together.'

I am taken by an intense feeling of joy. She smiles. She looks very young; she has a son, but she has escaped the ravages of childbirth. After childbirth Georgina became drawn; sleep deprivation manifested itself in the spaces under her eye sockets, where fine curlicues appeared. This ageing terrified her; she had been a model and minor actor when she was young. For Georgina no minor wrinkle could be tolerated. She patronised clinics in Switzerland, which administered Alpine plant extracts, she travelled to expensive plastic surgeons in America and she spent hours in the gym with a personal trainer. Lucinda was neglected when I went to my office in the City.

As a child she was left with a succession of nannies. It broke my heart when she called for her mother. Early on I understood that I was no more than the necessary husband, qualified only to bear witness to the sacred relationship of Madonna and Child, something which existed mostly in Georgina's mind. And it was then that I understood fully that she preferred image to reality in every possible way.

I have the comforting idea that Nellie and I can come even closer, that we can share our essences, even though I don't know how that would happen. I am aware that there is still something a little awkward in my expressions of love for Nellie, as though I am learning from a guidebook about a distant land, but I need to tell her how happy she has made me; I may be a little insistent in my neediness. I excuse myself on the grounds that what lovers say should be kept private for fear of ridicule.

Now Nellie is busy, making supper. She directs a smile my way. Her clothes and apron are pale blue and white. I have seen that blue is a colour Swedes cannot live without.

'Can I help you, darling?'

'It's fine,' she says. 'I am just making simple meatballs, Swedish style. Just as good as Ikea by the way.'

'I love them. I love meatballs. I love herring. I love Ikea. I love you. You are so kind. And so beautiful. Are you looking forward to Cape Town?'

'Yes, I am. I can't wait to get there and I am longing to see Lucinda again.'

'Lucinda will need you.'

'I know, but really, she needs you more.'

'I can't do it without you. I love her but she always manages to upset me.'

'We can handle it, I promise. She adores you and she knows what you have done for her. Now, are you hungry?'

'Always. We had no food as children. Just a bowl of mealie-meal once a day.'

'I feel so sorry for you. Poor you, it must have been terrible.'

'It was.'

'But you are not very thin now, are you?'

Nellie and I went together to California to deliver Lucinda to the clinic, and she and Lucinda have become close. Nellie has written to her or emailed her virtually every week since. She sometimes sends Lucinda articles she has found in papers, not spiritual stuff, but serious pieces by scientists and writers. I am happy to believe that the two of them have secrets that they don't share with me.

Nellie lifts the heavy lid of the casserole and looks at the meatballs; her face is wreathed in steam for a moment.

'Nearly ready. Frank, about Lucinda, you are her father. As I said, she adores you. But I will do my best.'

'I am relying on you. I can't do it alone, Nellie. I want to show you and Lucinda everything.'

'I want to know about where you come from. It will tell me a lot about you.'

She says 'lot' with a minor glottal explosion, which I find endearing.

I am not thinking of the sights, spectacular though they are. I want her to see why, for all its violence and poverty and corruption, I still have a powerful connection to South Africa, an irrational connection to the mountains and the landscape and the language. I could tell her about my ambivalence towards Piet Retief. I could tell her about my father fetching me from Tannie Marie's farm and how he and I wept in the Dodge, pulled over on the roadside. I could tell her that I left my tears in South Africa when my mother died and was buried in the churchyard of St Martin's in the Veld. And I could tell her that, when my father died, exiting characteristically politely, his ashes were buried in a small niche in the wall surrounding the churchyard where my mother is buried. This was as close as they had been for some years – my father had never visited the grave. He said visiting the church would cause him distress. I wondered if it was because of some lingering resentment to do with her lover.

I have been to the churchyard a few times. It is perfectly possible for an atheist to love churches and what they stand for, which is hope. I haven't told Nellie that I feel increasingly alien every day.

Now I feel an urge to go home, even if the home I have in mind is mostly imagined. I still think that my failed marriage is a disgrace, as if I were careless about these things. I am free now, but, like an escaped criminal, I often look behind me.

Last December when we were staying at the inn on Grinda in the Stockholm Archipelago, to celebrate the festival of Sankta Lucia, I saw what it meant to Nellie. It was not simply a question of nostalgia, as she suggested. Sankta Lucia celebrates light in the long northern winter. Young girls in white with candles in circlets on their heads processed into the church and sang traditional songs. Light and dark are represented by elves, both of the benign and the malevolent persuasion. There are plenty of creatures in Norse mythology that live a liminal existence, hovering between the spirit and the flesh-and-blood world. I think my Cousin Jaco imagines himself in a liminal world; even now he is somewhere roaming the universe with his special Scientologist's powers.

We travelled to Kiruna to see the Northern Lights swoop down almost to the ground, whirling restlessly, as if desperate to make land, to achieve some stability and permanence. Nellie said that the Sami believed that the lights are the souls of the dead looking for release. Children are required to act with respect to the departed when the aurora borealis fires the sky. On Grinda I was keenly aware that I didn't have a culture of my own and I was aware, too, that in South Africa people hold values and beliefs that are irreconcilable. Some whites have come to speak of themselves as 'white Africans' in an attempt to belong, but this is an affectation: very few of these people speak any African language or have any deep understanding of their black fellow countrymen and women.

'I suppose there must be wonderful fish in Cape Town,' Nellie says.

She gives the word 'suppose' a Swedish twist, as if it contains an extra, slippery consonant, ending in a gentle plop, like a seal sliding into water.

'Yes, there are fish, wonderful fish. We can go down to the harbour to buy tuna and lobster for nothing, straight off the boats.'

I am happily animating the idyll to come. It isn't the moment to tell her that, not too far from my house, my Cousin Jaco narrowly escaped being eaten by a great white shark.

In his incoherent emails, Jaco has taken to addressing me as 'Oom Frank', which I find intensely irritating from a man who is my remote cousin. He is in California, and has been designated a 'Clear', and now he is perfecting the skills that will allow him to visit Mars, propelled there only by mental forces – his. He says he has acquired the traffic-light skills already, so that he is able to change the traffic lights in his favour. No waiting for Jaco. I wonder if it isn't dangerous to have Jaco loose on Rodeo Drive – or on any other highway. All this he has told me in his confused and illiterate emails.

There are also intimations that his tales of shark encounters are beginning to lose traction; no television company or radio station has called him for months, despite the fact that quite a number of surfers have been attacked recently. Some of the survivors are willing to talk. Even a man with only one remaining leg is happy to tell the world about his experience. After the attack, his leg floated to the surface, and was seized by a second shark, never to be seen again.

Jaco emails to say that he is deep within the organisation, hush-hush, doing something important to secure his special powers and his immortality. And, although he is not supposed to speak to him,

Jaco tells me that he has met Tom Cruise, who is not as short as people say, and is a very nice person, more than willing to swap a few words with a fellow Scientologist. As Jaco puts it, Tom is his bru.

Outside it is dark. This is the primitive, rural version of dark, quite different from the fractured dark of the city. In the middle of the forest the darkness is intense; it has a texture that I imagine I can feel. The light spilling from the house is powerless up against the overwhelming night. The deer creep closer, in a nervous game of grandmother's footsteps. In the light spilled from a window, I can now see the white of their muzzles, as they come to the garden fence to graze. The bottom third of their muzzles is white as if they had drunk from a pail of milk. Their eyes glow. In the morning a few ponies will be waiting at the front door; against all advice I give them carrots. As soon as they see the house is occupied, they come for a hand-out. I own a few of the ponies on the forest, a right only a commoner can exercise. When I bought the house it included the right to run my own animals – excluding pigs – on the forest. I also have the right to gather and chop firewood; this is known as *estovers*. I have no plans to do anything with the ponies, but the knowledge that out there my four ponies are roaming happily, bearing my unique tail mark, gives me secret pleasure. The rights and duties are medieval in their origin. When I arrived in England I was eager to belong and that urge hasn't gone; I was happy to be away from turmoil and strife and from the endless, never-to-be-resolved, argument.

Nellie loves the trees and forest around us, possibly because so many Swedish myths have their origins in the forest. The Old

Norse word, *myrkviðr*, means murky or dark wood. It is deep in the Swedish psyche. Nellie is strangely pleased that we have the right of estovers, and that the wood scenting the house is our own. Here I sleep well: my dreams of drowning never assail me. I don't believe that dreams contain urgent messages or tidbits of wisdom or appraisals of the unconscious, but I wonder why my dreams are so vivid when I am in London.

Nellie and I sleep in sheets scented by lavender. We are cosseted by scents and freshness. I tell her that, years ago, the black women washed and dried our sheets on rocks in the Mooi River. I can't stop; I tell her that the women carried the bundles of clean clothes from the river, bound up in the sheets, balanced on their heads. I tell her I can see them now, walking in single file back from the river, singing in harmony. Nellie says she wishes she could see that; it would be a window on my childhood. She wants to know about me and the life I have lived.

She never passes judgement on Georgina, however vindictive she becomes. Nellie believes, and I agree with her, that no one ever really knows what happens within another's marriage. Her own marriage was happy; when Lars turned out to be a serious alcoholic she was devastated. She was angry when he said he had given up drinking. It was as though, Nellie told me, he no longer knew when he was lying: he mistook the intention for the action. He would arrive home at four in the morning, smiling pointlessly, ready to be forgiven, and she would have to drag him to bed after removing his urine- and drink-sodden clothes. Then he denied that he had been fired from his job as an engineer. Although she knew he was unable to quit drinking, she tried to persuade him to sign up for AA, but he never attended. They separated, reluctantly, and six months later they were divorced. He has terminal liver failure now and is often on dialysis. Everyone knows, says Nellie, that he will die soon. His face is yellow, signalling his death like a plague flag. I have seen pictures of Lars in his prime; Nellie's son, Bertil, is very like him – unmistakably a man of the far north. I ask questions about Lars sometimes but I avoid any hint of jealousy and I don't make comparisons.

A few months before I met Nellie, I had a brief relationship with a young woman, Imogen Cross, who was barely thirty.

We were sitting in a café. She asked me, 'Can we talk?'

'Of course.'

I sensed it would be one of those questions you know in advance is going to be painfully unanswerable.

She composed herself with difficulty. She said, 'Do we have a future?'

I was silenced for a moment; it had never occurred to me that we might have a future together. She seemed to be asking if we could spend the rest of our lives together and she suggested that I owed her something. I had treated sex with her as a kind of harmless entertainment and now I saw not a wonderful future so much as a middle-aged man parading a young wife and opening himself to all kinds of ridicule.

I wondered, for a start, how I would be able to introduce her to my friends. And it might have appeared to be lending credence to Georgina's widely advertised views of my lack of sensitivity, which she attributed to an early diet of biltong. In her view a meat diet is synonymous with brutish masculinity. She favours foodstuffs that have symbolic and spiritual qualities, so that quinoa is, in some unspecified way, good for you and soya milk contains a kind of innocence and salads are major cultural indicators. Many men don't take this seriously, in that way opening themselves to charges of wilfully inviting heart attacks and courting early senility. A friend said that, when he asked his wife what the point of salad was, she accused him of passive aggression. Salad as weapon.

As it happens, I have never liked biltong, although it has symbolic qualities for my countrymen. On the farm strips of meat, beef or game were soaked in brine for days before they were hung from a camel thorn tree in a small cage behind my Tannie Marie's house. The cage was like something you might use to house a canary, with smaller mesh. Flies had to be kept out, but circulating warm, dry air was required to dry the strips of meat. Hungry flies were always crawling over the mesh eyeing what was within. It put me off for ever.

I am thinking about all this as I walk across the forest before breakfast. It's another clear, cold day; in my mind my new happiness has made me a far more sensitive person. I worry that I may have been too harsh with Imogen. I told her we had no future at all, not because she wasn't a wonderful person et cetera, et cetera, but because I didn't want to ruin her life. I said I had far too much baggage, including a daughter who needed me. Imogen made some cutting remarks about using her. I assured her that it was not the case. She was married soon after to a man of her age who works in the City, and her tone has changed; she seems to be content. She has introduced me to her husband, perhaps as a kind of exorcism. His hair is gelled upwards at the front, in miniature stooks, a fashionable look for young men in retail banking.

Ahead of me is the little golf course. Ponies graze on the greens. The locals say you should try to land your ball right on the ponies' rumps; the ponies don't feel it, and the ball drops dead. One of the members claims to have had a hole in one after his ball bounced off a pony and into the cup. This may be a local myth. From here the course runs down to a point where the course drops away and emerges again at the other side of a clear stream.

Before I enter the house I can smell Swedish coffee – *mörkrost*, dark roast. Nellie hands me a cup.

'How was your walk?'

'Great. This is a wonderful time of the year. Actually I like the forest all year round.'

'Frank, good news, I just had a text from Bertil. He would love to come to Cape Town.'

'That's terrific, what a good idea. I am so glad. I have lots of space and he could learn to surf and all that stuff. It would get him out of himself a little. It could also be good for Lucinda to get to know him.'

'I am not sure he needs to get out of himself, but, yes, a happy holiday would be great.'

'Sorry. That's really what I was thinking about, his happiness. I think he has been a little down at times.'

'He takes Lars's problems to heart. He loves Lars, but seeing Lars is very difficult for him. It still makes me angry, as though he wanted to throw his life away. But I can't say that. In fact you are the only person I have ever told.'

'I think it could be good for Bertil and Lucinda to be thrown together. I hate to say it, but both of them are wounded and they need to be carefree.'

'It will be fine,' Nellie says reassuringly. 'They have a lot going for them.'

I am not sure just what it is that is going for them, but I have learned to trust Nellie's judgement in these matters. Still, I wonder if Bertil will accept that his mother is sleeping with me, although of course he knows already:

In the rank sweat of an unseamed bed,
Stewed in corruption, honeying and making love
Over the nasty sty.

There is something of the Hamlet about Bertil. He has been in my house in Notting Hill from his boarding school in Kent a few times and in his sullen withdrawal I saw a kind of passive resistance – perhaps not directed to me as a person, but to me as a substitute for Lars. There can be disgust and resentment in children whose parent has taken up with another.

For breakfast we have blueberry buttermilk pancakes and freshly gathered mushrooms on toast. We are going riding. I had my own horse, stabled near by, but he died of colitis last year. He was a lovely seven-year-old gelding – a bay – honest, even charming, and always eager. It was this eagerness that endeared him to me. His name was Bismarck when I bought him; I changed that to Rocket because I had read *My Friend Flicka* so avidly. I wanted to live in Wyoming.

As a boy in Johannesburg I used to ride during the school holidays; the high point of my holidays was always the Pony Club camp. About twenty children went to spend a week on a farm, riding our own ponies. The attraction was meeting girls, some of whom I later had sex with. As you get older your relationships with people you have slept with take on the aspect of something warm and innocent, something to be cherished, even if in reality the sex back then was casual and had some of the qualities of a treasure hunt.

Even now I can remember little details – the fine hairs on Jeanne Gallo's arms, Fran Cheesman's erotic teeth, Deborah Nutting's freckled nose and cheeks, with their endearing natural rain spots. Last year a friend emailed me to tell me that Deborah Nutting's first husband beat her up and she married again, to Dougie Nash, and he had a heart attack and died. Deborah emailed me: she has come through it all a stronger person. And she wants to meet up with me again.

Email has freed many people to rewrite their partial versions of their lives. Many of the emails sent to me are concerned with their highly successful children, who have emigrated from South Africa to Canada and Australia; they also tell of the struggles with life which have fortuitously revealed undiscovered artistic talent and self-sufficiency.

Nellie rides as she does everything – she is neat, uncomplicated and eager. In a way I am dreaming myself back into my Retief heritage: I ride like a Boer on commando, my feet thrust defiantly forwards. The horses are from our local stable. The stable girls looked after Rocket, and they were as upset as I was when he died. They still seem to think I need condolence. They talk to me in a solicitous whisper; they believe in the grieving process. I admire horsey people for their dedication, for embracing a world of mucking-out, tack cleaning, picking hooves, summoning vets, feeding and schooling the horses. In their minds I think the girls have the model of a kind of equine heaven. At the same time I feel that we patronise them as we sweep into the run-down and make-do yard in my Mercedes, where the horses are already saddled, waiting, resigned.

I once gave the owners a thousand pounds when they couldn't pay the feed bill. A truck was parked in the yard; the driver, who had long Victorian sideboards, said that the suppliers were not able to unload without payment. I took the company's details and made a payment by phone. The driver ordered his assistant, who was drinking a Lucozade, to unload. The driver said he was very sorry he had to put us in this position, but the high-ups in the firm insisted: since 2008 many people had been selling their horses or even giving them away. First thing to go in a recession, he said. Some of these horses ended up in curries or meat for hospitals, he said. He spoke with an almost lost accent, the Hampshire dialect, which was almost driven out by the Cockney influx to the new towns which were built forty years ago.

'We're 'anging on bouy the skin of've ow-er teeth,' he said.

It was beautiful to hear all those extra vowels. Like so many aspects of English life, they will be missed when they are gone for ever. I have a private sense of the country's increasing coarseness.

Nellie and I ride for an hour and a half. As we arrive at the old airstrip, unused since the war, the horses know what's coming: this is the gallop, the last hurrah. Off we go with a bound: soon my ears are cold and my nose is stinging as the horses' hooves thrum on the ground; this thrumming is one of the most thrilling sounds imaginable. And also one of the most feared in history. I think of cavalry charges in films and Cossack pogroms and country racecourses where you hear the horse-timpani rising from a distant hollow and coming ever closer until the horses themselves suddenly appear at the top of a hill, a mist escaping from them into the cold air.

On her first visit to the forest, Nellie introduced me to wild mushrooms; she spotted morels peering coyly from a hollow under beech trees. For her the natural world is a gift we must honour; it may be that up in the Nordic lands there is a more recent memory of the importance of relying on nature to survive. After all, the Vikings were the last pagans of Europe. When I dreamt of Nellie a few nights ago, I saw her in forests of spruce, weaving through the trees and leaving tracks in the snow. Nellie told me with pride that the oldest tree in the world, Old Tjikko, a spruce, is in Sweden. Over nine thousand years old. Beat that if you can.

Now the horses begin to slow down; soon they are trotting and then walking, at the same time snatching at their bridles in the eagerness to get home. I wonder sometimes how we came to enslave horses and other domestic animals. The somnolent sheep on my Tannie Marie's farm walked listlessly, heads down, like slaves, like inmates of a gulag.

Josie, one of the stable girls, is waiting. She holds the horses as we dismount. Her cheeks are very red – the redness is symmetrical, forming perfect red discs – like Victorian German dolls.

'Was he all right, Blaze?' Josie asks.

'Lovely. We had a great ride.'

'Nothing will replace Rocket.'

'No. And I wouldn't want it to.'

'He was a one-off.'

I am touched. The kindness of these girls, expressed through their concern for horses, moves me. I understood some time ago that many English people in the countryside see talking about their dogs or horses as a kind of overture to conversation, or even a ploy to avoid serious conversation.

Nellie takes my hand as we walk to the car. She wants to see the Rufus Stone. Not far from here, William Rufus, the son of William the Conqueror, was killed by an arrow in 1100 when he was hunting. His death was probably an assassination, the arrow fired by Walter Tirel on the orders of the King's brother, Henry, who succeeded to the throne.

The Rufus Stone purports to mark the exact spot where William Rufus was killed, but there is no certainty. The hunting party galloped away, leaving the body where it lay. The plaque reads:

Here stood the oak tree, on which an arrow shot by Sir Walter Tirel at a stag glanced and struck King William the Second, surnamed Rufus, on the breast, of which he instantly died, on the second day of August, anno 1100.

Nellie holds my hand insistently. Two hikers arrive, striding in blue and green cagoules, as though they are expecting a blizzard. The English love to dress up for a hike; outdoor clothing is popular in these parts. They say hello grudgingly, giving the impression that they think we have cheated by coming here in a car, without the requisite seriousness of purpose. I imagine that they think we are insensitive to the events of a thousand years ago. The man reads part of the inscription out loud, as if his wife can't read: '*King William the Second, surnamed Rufus, being slain as before related was laid in a cart belonging to one Purkis and drawn from here to Winchester and buried in the Cathedral Church of that city.'*

Purkis is a minor player in this drama, standing for the common man.

'History is so much about murder,' Nellie says.

From what I know of my ancestor's life, I would have to agree with her.

7

Nellie has to go to Kent to take Bertil home from school to pack and get ready. Bertil must have Vilebrequin swimming trunks; everybody at his school has them. I often see the shop in Piccadilly because it is next to a place that sells wonderful macaroons. I suggested Nellie should take my car, and I would take her Volvo to the garage for a service.

My phone rings.

'Yes.'

'Good, it's you, the hairy colonial. See how I have to scrape the barrel if I want some halfway decent conversation? I am dying of tedium. Ennui, as philosophers call it. It is so fucking boring in the country. Thank God you are here. Where's the lovely Nellie? Okay, I will have to make do with you. I can't stand living here. If I see another fucking dwarf pony I will run it over in my car. You wouldn't believe just how fucking dull it is. I should never have come to live here. If you don't have a dog or a horse or a fly rod, you might as well slash your wrists. The people in my village – it's literally mine – all talk about nothing except dogs and point-to-points and foxes. If you move one brick they rush round to English Heritage or the council to object. I don't think they would have a fucking clue how to conduct a conversation if they couldn't talk about their dogs or horses. They are always at the vet, laying out vast amounts of dosh. One woman I know spent a thousand pounds having a lesion removed from her parrot's beak. And then it fell off the perch. And when you get asked to dinner the food is always the same – something they have bodged up from the Waitrose recipe cards in Winchester. I have booked the Longdog for dinner tonight. Does that suit? Good, see you about 7.30.'

'Lovely. See you there, thanks.'

A few years ago my friend Alec sold his shares in his hedge fund and bought a country house and two farms. The rumour in the City was that he was pushed out. His house looks over the finest trout river in England, the Test, but after an initial burst of enthusiasm he decided he loathed fish and fishing. He said he hated seeing the beautifully marked but brainless creatures gasping on the bank. Also he thinks that all the florid fishing lore that was developed in the area is complete nonsense – woo-woo. And one more thing, he thinks trout are inedible. They taste of damp laundry, he says.

He tried golf but he gave that up too; he hadn't realised it was so difficult. Particularly with all those fucking ponies wandering about the course. The truth is he was at his happiest wheeling and dealing in the City and now he is missing the life. He is said to have helped a private bank avoid bankruptcy in 2009 with some unorthodox financial manoeuvres, and he made another ten million when the bank recovered. He was eased off the board and only a few months later Lavinia died; without knowing, she had been harbouring a virulent brain tumour for some years. It grew like a giant onion. She had loved visiting all the classic gardens in the south of England, and Alec would go along, sulking loudly, but after her death he could not cope and suffered depression for months.

I am more than happy to have dinner with him. He didn't like Georgina – many people have told me this since our divorce – but there may be equal numbers who say the same of me to her supporters. Sometimes they are disparaging about my origins, as though there is something half-formed about South Africans, a certain crudity. African tribes believe that the hyena is so ugly because when God made them he ran out of clay, condemning the hyena to a sloping back and a furtive manner. In this way, some people think there is something comical, even deficient, about South Africans.

Alec gave me my first job when I arrived in England. He was starting up a stockbroking firm. I had dropped out of Oxford, a fact that Alec never mentioned. He introduced me to all his clients: 'Frank McAllister, Oxford man, colonial unfortunately, but it can't be helped.'

In the beginning Alec paid me £60 a week to answer the phone to his clients and then to engage these clients with my playful and caressing manner; Alec believed that that was the hallmark of an Oxford man. He made me a partner after a year and for the first time I had some money. We parted very amicably four years later and I went to work in a property company, which was a good time to be in property. Houses could be bought and cheaply renovated; it was then that I met Georgina, who was thinking of setting up a small hotel. She thought I was the foreman, which in a sense I was. I could only afford to pay one full-time bricklayer.

Alec loves Nellie. She seems to appeal to all my friends. I am sure they wonder what she sees in me.

★

The Longdog has been painted in fashionable Farrow & Ball colours recently. I like these colours; we have used them in the house. I am early, so I walk out to the river for a few minutes. The trout are rising, sipping at the water. Just on the bend of the river someone is fishing, almost as though he had been put there to complete the picture.

Alec arrives. He is wearing narrow, strawberry-coloured trousers, so drawing attention to his waistline, which has gone freelance. On his finger he has a large signet ring. Since he left the City, he no longer creates much of an eddy in a confined space. I haven't ever fully understood him, although I have come to see that, underneath the commotion, he is a kind man. We often talk about our children. He has three, all of whom are nightmares, according to him. One of his, a boy, took drugs and it was Alec who told me about the place in California. We sit at his special table and he begins a sort of interrogation-cum-flirtation with the waitress, who is young and nervous, with a soft, innocent face.

'When it says "burrata"' – he stabs the menu with his forefinger – 'is that really what you have? Not just some two-week-old mozzarella made in a factory in Basingstoke and dunked in water?'

There is an insistent and disturbing quacking tone in his voice.

'I'll ask the chef, sir.'

'Don't worry, I will have the burrata and heritage tomatoes for a starter. Sweetbreads for a main. Oh, maybe, before you vanish, can you tell me something: what does "heritage" mean in this context? No? I can tell you, it means bollocks, designed for the gullible. And you, Frankie, what are you going to have?'

'Steady Alec, you're making her anxious.'

Alec is the only person who calls me Frankie. The waitress scuttles off with our order, probably hoping not to be brought before the inquisition again.

'So what's happening in your life? Are you okay, dear man?'

'I'm fine, Alec. Me, Nellie, her son, Bertil, and Lucinda are going to Cape Town to my house for a month or more. Will you come for a week or so?'

'I need a break. I haven't had a decent holiday since I don't know when.'

'Oh please, you were in Croatia on somebody's boat for two weeks, look at you, still as brown as a nut, then you were in New York and the Hamptons, and then you went skiing.'

'Yes, and then I fell all the way down the fucking Vallée fucking Blanche. I am lucky to be alive. I ended up in a crevasse, fortunately not too deep. The guide laughed. He asked me if I had seen any fish down there. *La pêche est bonne?* An old Alpine joke, apparently. I wanted to kill him, but as he was lowering a rope to pull me out, I kept quiet.'

'How's Jacqui? Still seeing her?'

'Not often. In fact not at all.'

He lowers his voice: 'She is a sex fiend. Terrifying. I felt I had to go to the gym before she came over. And the gorgeous Nellie, is she as wonderful as always?'

'She's changed my life. Really. I know, I know what you are thinking. The truth is Georgina dragged me down over the years – perhaps I dragged myself down – but I was unhappy a lot of the time. It is as if Nellie is the polar opposite of Georgina. By the way, do you know Georgina is trying to have a baby?'

'Turkey-baster job, I hear.'

'If by that you mean *in vitro* fertilisation administered by some incredibly posh gynaecologist in Harley Street – yes, it's a turkey-baster job. The worst thing is that my best man's friend has donated his sperm. It makes me sick to think about it.'

I feel guilty for going along with broadcasting this potential tragedy. A tragedy in waiting, mostly for Georgina, I think. She is not one of the world's natural mothers. She wants the credit for being a mother without really liking children or wanting her life to be disrupted.

'It's probably better that he delivered the sperm in a glass tube through a hatch,' Alec says, 'rather than by the old-school method. Look, just don't think about it. It's a way – admittedly a rather Byzantine way – of getting at you.'

At this moment the burrata arrives. Under the circumstances it has a gynaecological look as it sits limply on a plate. Alec is silent and absent for a moment. His face is drained of life, and it has a chalk-white dryness I haven't seen before, as though his human essences have dried up and he has become the outline of what was once a ruthless businessman. He has lived his whole life believing that England is a kind of sceptred isle, but now he blames the country for his decline. As if to confirm that a certain creeping tackiness has entered his life, I have heard that he is having a relationship with a lap dancer, which is just the sort of thing that will certainly end in disaster.

'Are you okay, Alec?'

'Sorry, old boy. I have low blood pressure, and it comes on when I think of Lavinia. You know I am in a new relationship?'

'I heard you had taken up with a lap dancer.'

'She's a sweet girl, a student, filling in time as lap dancer, and I am helping her get to university. She wants to be an anthropologist.'

'Jesus, are you sure you haven't made this up? What's your role? To pay her tuition fees?'

'Frank, listen, I'm sorry to throw up on your shoes, but I feel completely lost. I know I am making a complete arse of myself. She's Latvian by the way. From Riga.'

'Oh good, that makes all the difference. The Latvians are the aristocrats of the Baltic.'

'Don't, please. I never expected to be this lonely and so lacking in self-esteem and generally so ridiculous. One week after leaving the board I was a forgotten man. And also I just somehow never bargained for being ousted or for Lavinia's death.'

He looks terrible – etiolated and wilting. His whole aspect has changed; the former titan of finance has become one of those men who lose their dignity and their dress sense soon after they lose office and try to demonstrate that they are still in the game. Some of them take to wearing broad felt hats and jaunty caps from Jermyn Street, which never rest naturally on old people. I am guessing that his liaison with a Baltic lap dancer was intended to suggest youthfulness, but his clothes carry a different message, one of desperation. His hair, I now see, has been dyed, which is seldom a good idea for middle-aged and elderly men. Just beneath his ears, his hair has become unevenly ginger, where once it was greying. His ears have an inquisitive look, as they poke out – questing fungi – from under his Icelandic-pony-coloured hair.

Alec is so sombre by the time he climbs into his Jaguar, with the help of his chauffeur, that I fear for him. He lives not far away in an ugly pile with fifteen bedrooms. Like many people who have been successful in business, he believes he has talent as a designer. He is wrong, the house is a jarring mishmash. His children apparently avoid him, and the house. I wonder if the lap dancer is waiting for him there now.

As I drive home to the forest I think about what Alec said about his state of mind. Is this what waits for us all, a kind of cruel humiliation in old age? It is frightening how fragile a life can be; a paper-thin divide separates one life from another, one fate from another, one choice from another. There is no certainty, no fulfilment. All is arbitrary. All is ultimately darkness.

When I arrive at the house, deep in the ancient wood, I see the light I left on as a beacon of hope, spilling out onto the path to the front door. Two ponies are lying down just beyond the garden fence. Their comfortable outlines are blurred as though they had been drawn with a soft charcoal pencil.

As I enter the house I find that my phone is signalling a message. I don't recognise the American number. Who would call at this time of night? It might be Lucinda. I go to voicemail. Someone, a man, is crying. It's painful. Then I hear my name. '*Oom Frank, Oom Frank, waar is jy? Asseblieftog, Oom, ek het jou nood.*'

It is my Cousin Jaco: in Afrikaans he is begging me to help him. Maybe he doesn't want others to know what he is saying. But now he breaks into English. It takes me a moment to realise he is talking about the Scientologists.

'Oom, they say I may only leave the church by paying $75,000 which is the fees what my training have cost. They is crazy. I am in deep shit, Oom. Can you send this money to their lawyers in Los Angeles, please, please? I will pay you back even if I must work to the end of my life. I promise. I make you a covenant, on the name of Piet Retief. You must please call this number in LA.

It is the lawyer who negotiate this kind of thing. *Asseblieftog*, Frank.'

'Okay, give me the number.'

I am not persuaded by his evocation of Piet Retief as guarantor. Jaco reads the number, stumbling. He is deeply distressed; his voice has an unstable and snivelling content. I try the phone number and get through to a lawyer's office. It is called Asphalter and Gersbach.

I say that I am calling on behalf of my cousin, Mr Jaco Retief, who is apparently being prevented from leaving the Church of Scientology.

'I don't think that is correct, Mr … What did you say your name is? Right, Mr McAllister, that is not true, one hundred per cent wrong.'

'Cut the bullshit. My cousin believes he can only leave by making a payment.'

'We don't tolerate foul language. Please don't violate our office again. Your cousin is in arrears with the money he owes to the Church for their teaching over nearly sixteen months and also for accommodation.'

'Do you or don't you want to be paid?'

'I will put you through to Mr Asphalter. Just one moment please, sir.'

After a minute or two, Asphalter answers.

'Yes, sir. I believe you are the cousin of Mr Jaco Retief?'

'Yes, that is true. Look, he says he has to pay to be allowed to go, and he has asked me to help.'

'Your cousin is not being prevented from leaving. He is simply being asked not to jump ship until his financial commitments are fulfilled.'

'He is on a ship? Is that what you are saying?'

'No, sir, he is not on a ship. It's an American saying, "jumping ship". It means deserting.'

'I know what it means. I speak English. But I also happen to know that your organisation did in fact have some ships. Before you say any more, let me tell you I am certainly your only chance of getting paid to release my cousin from your church, where presumably he was attempting to achieve enlightenment.'

'Firstly, Mr McAllister, I am a lawyer. I act for the Church of Scientology in that capacity. I wouldn't know if your cousin was seeking enlightenment.'

'Listen up, I am only going to say it once. I am prepared to send you $50,000 within a few hours as long as you can bring my cousin to the phone when the money is transferred to your bank account, so that he can confirm that he has been released.'

' "Discharged his commitments" would be our preferred description over "released".'

'Have you understood a word I said? I am not bargaining; no one on this planet is going to ransom Jaco Retief, except me, and this is your one and only chance to cash in. He must be in your office, standing next to you, in an hour. You can call me in the next ten minutes to inform me if my offer is accepted. And just in case you have forgotten, I am only prepared to pay $50,000.'

'Just one thing, sir, this is not ransom.'

'Please. Call it whatever you like.'

Ten minutes later Asphalter calls to say that my offer is accepted. I tell him to call when he has Jaco in his office. An hour later he calls: Jaco is now in the office. He is tearful, overcome with emotion. I call Coutts & Co. in London and give them the details. The transfer will be complete within a few hours.

'Thank you, Oom.'

'Jaco, please, enough of this "Oom" stuff. What are you going to do now?'

'I am going home. I can't wait. My girls is growing up and my wife has a new partner, he's a life coach. *Ek moes huistoe gaan*. I must go home.'

'That's probably a good idea. Don't join any cults.'

'No, I won't be doing that in a hurry, that's for sure. Oom, one little thing' – he uses the Afrikaans diminutive, '*dingetjie*' – 'can you pay for my plane ticket to Jo'burg?'

'Okay, but don't ask me for anything ever again. And listen, next time I will be rooting for the shark.'

Jaco laughs after a short silence, but the laugh has a strangled tone, and his voice is painfully hoarse.

The bank calls; the transfer will be with the law office of Asphalter and Gersbach within a few hours. When the bank confirms that the draft has cleared, Jaco will be turned loose on the world.

It's dawn before I get to bed. I don't sleep well. My mind is disturbed.

Even more disturbing is the fact that Jaco seems to think that I am his creator, his Geppetto.

8

I will calm down as soon as we are on the plane to Cape Town. I always look forward to the first sighting of Table Mountain, lapped by the sea. The moment the crew opens the plane's doors I will inhale the perfume of the local *fynbos*, which people from the Cape find intoxicatingly sweet; I am one of them, although my relationship with these scents is complex; they soothe me but they also remind me painfully of boarding school. Scents can summon powerful memories of love and nostalgia and fear. This scent also recalls memories of my father, who claimed that the *fynbos* was health-giving, a free stimulant, a pick-me-up, floating about in the air. He also believed in the benefits of sea water as therapy. He found physical contact and affection difficult. All the same, he was a decent man, but too conventional to my youthful and cynical eye.

My father belonged to a generation that did not want to be conspicuous. He played golf in a V-necked pullover and a tie. He wore pinstriped suits in the heat of Johannesburg, suits made by Nelson Mandela's tailor, Yusuf Surtee, who also made suits for the mining magnates. That was in the time before Mandela's colourful ethnic shirts ousted the tailored suit.

My father's conventionality sprang, I think, from the devastating fact that his father had died when he was only fourteen and his mother became an alcoholic who had to be locked away. Ever after my father was looking for approval and endorsement. He was a widely respected journalist and received awards in many countries for his crusading journalism and this acknowledgement calmed his insecurity.

As soon as I first heard the word, I saw myself as a *flâneur*, roaming the streets of Paris, London and Rome. I roamed all of these, and more. I slept in a phone box in Paris and under an upturned fishing boat in Ostia; I hitch-hiked around America; I had a love affair with a contessa in Rome and I was deported from Tunisia, because I had no visa.

As I lie on my bed with the night-sounds of the forest for company, these things go through my mind as if on a loop. I think of my father in his fawn jersey; of the wind blowing in over the sea from the south-east, propelling the sand of Muizenberg to the squatter camps where the wind launches the detritus into flight, sending it towards the Atlantic coast. The detritus consists mostly of plastic bags, flying urgently away on a mission, or perhaps fleeing. My mother found these scenes disturbing; she reacted as if plastic bags were souls fleeing, as if every bag contained the avatar of a child who had died of hunger or some obscure illness of poverty. I think of the entrancing, inescapable, mysterious, overwhelming mountain, a natural cathedral rising out of the city and its suburbs, a cathedral which looks as if its towers have not yet been finished for lack of funds; I think of the sea rolling non-stop onto the endless beach of False Bay; I think of the great white shark menacing Jaco with its rows of frightening, clinical teeth. Jaco's fate could have been worse than Piet Retief's but for the whimsical and choosy nature of this particular shark. I see Piet Retief sitting down with Dingane in anticipation of the fatal dance, of his eager expectation of how these kaffirs will jump and posture and exclaim, like large children. And I wonder how the Reverend Francis Owen could have watched the killing. Was his life blighted for ever? Did he see it as a vision of hell? The ninth ring of Inferno?

History will always be a mystery, never fully trustworthy, never wholly or fully understood by those who come after. History is a narrative written for a purpose – for any number of purposes – but it is seldom able to convey the essence of being human. It is difficult enough to understand these things in your own time and place.

Finally I sleep, and when I wake the ponies have gone and the morning is calling urgently. Alone in my house I am wondering if I really did speak to Jaco and, if I did, whether it wasn't perhaps some sort of scam to get his hands on my money. It's possible that Mr Asphalter, Attorney at Law, is a fiction. 'Attorney at Law' – how sonorous, how pompous, the legal profession is. My battles with Georgina exposed me to many of the high-altitude crooks who always opened a meeting with a little unsolicited eulogy devoted to themselves and a litany of their many accomplishments, including their first-class degrees at Oxford and their many prizes from the Inns of Court. All through a conference in Gray's Inn, the barrister I was consulting walked around his antique chambers, describing to me his successes as a divorce specialist. I felt I was there only to admire him, when what I wanted was his plan of action to bring my torture to an end.

There is a direct line from the law to absurdity. He was probably unaware as he promenaded around his chamber that he was not as different from Dickens's comical lawyers as he would have liked to believe.

I see Jaco's number on my phone; other details of the night surface in my memory, so that I have to accept that I didn't dream that I had sent $50,000 to get Jaco away from the Scientologists. I should perhaps have made a donation to ensure that he stayed where he was a little longer and worked on his ability to fly to Mars. Or any other planet and star other than ours.

I walk on the forest for an hour in the stillness of the early morning. The animals are stunned by the night and are just getting their bearings; the deer are somnolent and pensive and the cattle lie comfortably under the trees. The early sunlight filters down through the mist clinging to the trees; it lacks only Merlin, in Burne-Jones's painting, to capture the mystic past. The ponies, perhaps because of the advance of the pint-sized stallions, are anxious, and maybe excited, as if a Viking longboat has landed and is about to get on with the rapine.

Bertil's housemaster calls to say that he is obliged to tell all the parents that some of the year elevens in his house have been caught smoking marijuana. One boy has been expelled. He says that it is possible that Bertil may have been smoking marijuana.

'Are you really worried?' I ask.

'No. Not seriously worried. But the marijuana available is much more potent than it used to be. I thought I should tell you. I am speaking to all the parents in year eleven. I am very sorry this should have happened.'

'What should I tell his mother?'

'Well perhaps you should just keep a watch for drugs. By the way Bertil is a very able boy. He's not one of the ringleaders and this is only an alert.'

'I am sure it will be fine when he gets to Cape Town with us,' I say. 'And we will look out. Thanks for calling.'

In South Africa hash was called 'dagga' and we all smoked it during the school holidays. We also drank cheap brandy, so I am not really qualified to advise. I notice that the housemaster hasn't given me the latest information, which is that regular dope smoking, particularly of skunk, alters the structure of the brain, and does not steer us towards a better understanding of our world; in fact it sends heavy users in the direction of a narrow, reduced, world of paranoia and depression and agoraphobia. And the damage can be permanent.

I call Nellie to tell her about what the housemaster has said. She says immediately that she will talk to Bertil and explain that there can be no drugs because of Lucinda.

'I am sure – well – I hope,' I say to Nellie, 'that he will get caught up with surfing and so on. I have already booked a lodge for a few nights on a reserve not far away, where we can fish and swim and see plenty of animals: antelope and wild cats, tortoises, baboons, snakes and zebras. It wouldn't be good for Bertil or for Lucinda to smoke dope there.'

'No, that's right. As I said, I will talk to him about it. I know he's sensible after all. He will understand.'

'I'm sure he is. And he has had a lot to contend with.'

I am saying these things, which I can't possibly corroborate, because I see myself as responsible for everyone's happiness. I want all of us to be happy and relaxed. The last thing I need is to have Lucinda taking up marijuana again with Bertil.

Nellie and I go over the arrangements about meeting at Heathrow. I have the tickets. She and Bertil and Lucinda will meet me there, and so on … all the minutiae of travel, which have become so tedious. Liz, my secretary, has done all the work.

I give Nellie an account of my dealings with Jaco last night. She's shocked: she finds it hard to believe that a church could behave like this. It's just not conceivable. But then she's thinking Lutheran Christianity. I tell her what L. Ron Hubbard wrote about flying to Mars under your own steam, achieved by harnessing your mental powers. I do it to give her an indication of the discourse in the Church of Scientology.

'Poor Jaco, is he all right?'

'Yes, and he is heading for South Africa. He wants to go home for ever. He thinks he may have strayed too far from his roots and I think he's probably right.'

'Don't be unkind. He has had a terrible ordeal.'

And it's cost me $50k.

'He has had a hard time, but he is a lightning rod for disaster. My advice is, don't stand near him in a storm.'

In the evening we are gathered at Heathrow, apart from Lucinda, who has not arrived as planned. Her text says she is coming to Cape Town a couple of days later. She gives no reason. She will text me her flight details when she has them. I try to suppress the fear that she may be as unreliable and erratic as ever. Bertil is silent, but Nellie says he is very happy to be going to South Africa. I wonder if she will be the interpreter of his inner feelings. He is wearing narrow jeans and bright blue trainers with a shiny, laminated look. He is already as tall as his mother. We have a brief conversation; he wants to know if he can have surfing lessons.

'Absolutely. We will get you all you need, and an instructor. Below the house the water can be very cold, depending on the currents and the wind, but over on the other side, the Indian Ocean side, it is always warm and you can stay in all day.'

'Great. Thanks, Frank.'

He has a steady gaze, perhaps still a little narrowed by grief; his eyes are some distance above his mouth; his nose bridges the gap. His forehead is wide and in this respect too he is very like his father. Also, strangely, they both resemble Alfred Nobel, who accidentally blew up many of his family members and in this way leaving himself lonely and single by the time he was fifty.

Morning reveals a beautiful view of Cape Town; the sea is streaming around Table Mountain, and the mountain is lightly and gently attended by wispy cloud. As the plane heads obligingly close to the city, I point out Robben Island, lying flat on the sea like a ragged green-and-brown fragment of carpet. I feel duty-bound to adopt the role of tour guide: Robben Island means Seal Island, and there are penguins on the island; the water is freezing; it's 4.2 miles from the mainland; nobody has ever escaped; Nelson Mandela was imprisoned there for eighteen years.

As the plane banks in a great arc, I point out Devil's Peak and the cable station. We bank more sharply and turn north over the sea, wheeling in from False Bay and crossing its twenty-mile beach before losing height; miles of shacks and squatter camps, also known as informal settlements, come into view. The new South

Africa favours these anodyne changes of name. A wag once described stealing from whites as 'affirmative shopping'.

We drive in a hire car towards the mountain, sweeping by the shacks, then passing close to the docks before rising up towards the Malay quarter with its many-coloured cottages and its small mosques, as we head up towards the pass leading out of Cape Town and down towards the Atlantic. The view as we arrive at the top of the pass is breathtaking. Down below are the Atlantic and the village of Camps Bay, with its perfect beach. I indicate to Bertil the best surfing, Glen Beach at the northern corner of the main beach. I feel proprietorial. Every time I make this drive my spirits soar. The village itself is surrounded by the *fynbos*, and I take in its scents eagerly. How persistent these ancient and irrational attachments are.

'You didn't tell me just how beautiful this place is,' says Nellie.

'I tried. But you have to see it for yourself.'

We drive down from the mountain to sea level. Surfers are out at Glen Beach. I used to surf there as a boy. Nothing has changed; I remember every rock. The road is not far above the waves. Sometimes sea spray sweeps across the road. The sea is relatively quiet today. In lay-bys, Africans are selling wooden giraffes and masks and Dogon doors and carpets and zebra skins. Behind them is a glorious seascape. On the mountain side, the houses end abruptly and the mountain wilderness reasserts itself. There are baboons and green Cape cobras in this dense *fynbos* and in the deep forests that line the ravines. These cobras are venomous; their poison can kill a dog in a few minutes.

I pull over to point out a pod of southern right whales, cruising up the coast towards some mysterious destination. Capetonians see whales as a compliment to them, as if they and the whales are in partnership, exchanging vital knowledge, not accessible to outsiders.

'I can't believe this,' says Nellie. 'I have never seen anything so, so incredibly beautiful.'

She seeks agreement from Bertil in Swedish. I hear the word '*vacker*', beautiful.

Bertil raises his eyebrows and gives me a look, which I take, happily, to be complicity. I remember just how critical fourteen-year-olds are of their parents, as if they are waking up to their failings for the first time. I take this as a good sign, evidence of bonding. I remember specifically how touchy Lucinda could be with me and her mother in public. How fervently you want your children to be happy, and how readily they will renounce you.

The road rises sharply now. Halfway up, we turn off and descend towards the sea on a narrow, winding road leading to the beach. My house is at the bottom of the road. We pull up in front of the house. I have the remote control and the gates open. The house looks directly down onto huge rocks of granite, where the Bushmen, the Khoisan, once lived. And a boy drowned. An enormous midden of shellfish in a cave is the proof. These people were the *strandlopers*, the beach-walkers, who foraged along the beaches and the bays. Piet Retief's Hottentot boys were *voorloopers*, those who walked ahead on the doomed march into Zululand.

My house is called Menemsha, after a fishing village on Martha's Vineyard. I drive the car down directly into the garage under the house. It has a sophisticated security system. From the road you reach the front door of the house by crossing a small ravine on a bleached wooden boardwalk. Down below the sea is roaring.

Lindiwe is waiting for us. I see that she is wearing her best shoes and housecoat. I am touched. Her face is a little more creased. Her husband was murdered recently and I have been supporting her. Her house is miles away in the townships on the windy flatlands out of town, near the airport, and it is dangerous to travel there and back every day in the taxi-buses. I have had a bedroom and sitting room added on to my house for her and she says she is very happy. Still, she takes her days off in the townships. There, women beg for the discarded intestines of cows from butchers, cutting them into lengths like socks, and cleaning them in the open before cooking them to sell by the road. Here we eat Cape rock lobster and tuna. Two worlds are living side by side. Nellie is alert to inequality; after all she is Scandinavian.

I hug Lindiwe, ignoring her embarrassment.

'Lindi, I want you to meet Nellie, and this is her son Bertil.'

Lindiwe gives every appearance of being pleased to see us.

'Welcome, madam,' she says to Nellie, holding one of her wrists while shaking hands in the traditional way with the other, as if readying herself for a two-handed tennis stroke.

'Welcome, Master Bertil.'

'Please call me Nellie and my boy, Bertil.'

Lindiwe smiles, but I know this is not really negotiable.

'Lindi has worked for me since I built this house five years ago. She runs the place, don't you, Lindi?'

'I am trying, sir.'

She will never be able to shake off the deep deference she was taught. To her I am security and reliability; in African custom I am the big man who looks after his extended family. Like President

96

Zuma. I love her for her loyalty and her kindness. She is also shrewd, making sure that everything runs smoothly.

'Sir, where is Miss Lucinda?'

She pronounces 'where is' as 'whez-a'.

'Oh, she is coming very soon. There has been a delay.'

'Is she a big girl now?'

'Yes, she is twenty-two years old.'

'How! She has twenty-two years already. She muss be beautiful now. She will have a husband.'

Lindiwe has had troubles of her own and God knows what horrors she has seen; she wanted to leave the townships after her husband died because of the numbers of young people on *tik*, crystal meth. They would kill anybody for a mobile phone and kill anybody's enemy for less than two thousand rand, something like one hundred pounds. Her husband was hit on the head with a litre bottle of Coca-Cola and robbed of his wages. He died in the back of the ambulance.

All the bedrooms are made up with fresh linen; there are flowers from the garden everywhere and the pool is crystal clear. The pool guy is a coloured man who lost his job as a clerk in the municipality, and took up swimming pools. He has a pick-up, a *bakkie*, and will transport plants and building materials. He's Afrikaans-speaking, and his name is Frikkie. His face is a record of his previous drinking habits. Now that he is dry, he goes to the Watchtower Bible and Tract Society near the harbour for reassurance.

I show Nellie and Bertil around. Nellie is entranced by the house; she thinks it certainly does have a Martha's Vineyard look, all painted wood floors and gentle, Baltic colours of blue and white. Bertil appears to like his room and shower right at the top, a sort of crow's nest with a small balcony and views all the way to Argentina. Skeins of sea birds fly low over the water through the burnt-umber light. Now ships are passing purposefully some way out; at this time of year the whales are close to the shore, sending us fraternal greetings as they pass. The light falls quickly and as a result the cormorants are always in a hurry to roost. There is something sensible and well-drilled about them.

My bedroom – our bedroom – has the advantage of being as far from Bertil's as possible; it has its own, private terrace beyond the room. One side of the terrace looks down onto the indigenous scrub and a small stream. By the pool, under a tree, Lindiwe has laid out the tea and a cake. It's her speciality, granadilla cake – passion fruit – and there is no question of refusing. She has observed that white people must have cake, often.

I am anxious about Bertil and how he is going to react. I tell him he is more than welcome to have a swim in the pool and that we have some wetsuits he can try for size if he wants to swim in the sea, but he should only do that if the lifeguards are on duty. Nellie gives him the parcel that holds the Vilebrequin cozzie. He opens it; the cozzie is adorned with a design of dark red lobsters and green palm trees.

'Thanks, it's really cool,' Bertil says.

'How about a kiss for your mother?'

'Okay. If I have to.'

The water, I tell him again, is often very cold here on the Atlantic side – our side – of the mountain and the riptide can be frightening. When I first came here I nearly drowned. Down below a few boys and one girl are surfing in increasingly tumultuous waves. It's heroic; they lie on the boards paddling hard, and duck through ten-foot waves until they are three hundred yards off shore and they come storming back towards the beach, carving down the face of the wave or riding the tubes. The search for the perfect wave drives them on with a fervour; they can't stop because the next wave may be absolutely perfect, unique – the second coming. It's an addiction.

Bertil watches the surfers closely.

'We will fix you some lessons for tomorrow, Bertil.'

'Thanks, Frank, that would be great.'

The three of us walk down to the beach, which is almost deserted; stilts and avocets are still fussing at the far end of the beach and a woman is walking two English setters; using a sort of catapult, she throws a tennis ball into the waves for the dogs to fetch, which they do eagerly; they were born to this life.

Two lifeguards sit on the boardwalk outside their hut, kissing. The boy has long blond hair. I know the girl: she is embarrassed to see me under these circumstances. She is only fourteen. She is wearing red shorts and a sort of singlet – life-savers' kit. I introduce her to Bertil and Nellie. The boy walks away as we approach, ostentatiously using his binoculars to see how the surfers are faring, as if snogging Vanessa Ovenstone was just a passing diversion, nothing to do with his main work, which is to prevent surfers and swimmers from drowning themselves.

'Can you surf?' Vanessa asks Bertil.

'Not yet,' he says, 'but I would like to learn.'

'I can help you to get started tomorrow: the wind is going to change and the water will be warmer.'

'Thanks, that would be great.'

With her enthusiasm she is making up for being caught kissing the boy with the long hair.

'Where you guys from?' she asks Nellie.

'We are Swedish, although we live in England. Bertil is at school in England. But this is something special; this is paradise. I want to live here,' Nellie says.

'*Ja*, it's pretty good, isn't it? Maybe a bit samey if you live here all the time. I better go, I am supposed to be on duty.'

'Lovely to see you again, Vanessa,' I say.

She is golden brown, her hair bleached by the sun. I think she may never be this beautiful again. She turns to me.

'How long are you staying, Mr McAllister?'

'Nothing is fixed. Bertil has five weeks off. So we will see. Will you tell your mum we are back? And we would like to see your parents.'

'For sure.'

She jogs down the beach.

'Sweet child,' says Nellie. 'She looks very young. Is she a lifeguard herself?'

'She is training; these kids were brought up here, they can all swim like fishes. Being a lifeguard is very glamorous. And there are perks. But believe me, they know how to use buoyancy aids or paddle boats if things get rough out there.'

'Pretty girl,' says Nellie.

Bertil grimaces at this maternal intervention. Mothers are incontinent with their opinions. He watches Vanessa walking along the shore, her feet in the water. She looks back and gives us a wave. Bertil waves in return, bloodlessly. I am hoping that Vanessa and Bertil will become friends. I have a mission to bring us all together, to find some sort of happiness for Lucinda – which would assuage my guilt – and ditto for Bertil. I want him to like me, even to love me, but I must go slowly. I have a tendency to be overbearing. At least that was Georgina's widely published opinion. But I am aware that I have brought them all here and I am responsible for their safety. Lucinda sends me a text: she is now due to arrive in two days' time. She gives me the flight number. There is no apology or explanation for the delay.

We have a late lunch on the terrace. Lindiwe is rushing about; there is watermelon and winter melon on the table, coronation chicken, Lindiwe's speciality, on a huge pale blue platter commissioned for the house from a local potter, and there are piles of lobsters, fresh from the boats, served with home-made mayonnaise and after that home-made rum-and-raisin ice cream. I see that it is a ritual, a celebration. I think that the sun's warmth and the sea's mysterious insistence below us are already forming us and siphoning off the residual anxieties of travel and dislocation. I have an overwhelming feeling of well-being. Nellie squeezes my hand and whispers, 'Thank you.' Bertil notes this, but he too seems to have succumbed to the promise of happiness.

After lunch we take a rest; we are jet-lagged and we have as much time as we want. In our room Nellie and I make love silently; I am seized by the idea that there is something of profound meaning at stake.

Nellie whispers, 'To love someone is to aim for one soul and one body. That's what you said, *min hjärtat.*'

We are close together, slightly moist, her breasts pressed against my chest.

'It may sound impossible and I know it is corny, but that's what I believe. You have to remember, I am just a simple Boer.'

'Oh, of course you are. I forgot. And you know, I like corny.'

We sleep deeply, as one.

Suddenly there is a screaming and the crashing of chairs turning over outside. I run towards the garden with a towel around my waist. Two male baboons are fighting for the remains of our lunch, retrieved from the bins. One baboon is holding the shell of a lobster as it gallops across the terrace and leaps over the table. It turns suddenly, its huge yellow teeth bared, menacing the other baboon, which backs off. Then it runs and jumps nimbly off the terrace and into a tree, still clutching the exoskeleton of the lobster as Lindiwe arrives with a broom and shouts at the baboons in Xhosa.

'What was that?' Nellie asks as she appears cautiously in her robe.

'Just two baboons. There they are, in those trees. We are open to the bush and forest on this side. But they don't often come our way, don't worry. I keep a catapult just in case they get a little bit presumptuous. I like them actually: they are highly intelligent, but a little low rent. All I have to do is pretend to use the catapult and they are off.'

'Are they dangerous?'

'Not really. They sometimes attack dogs and they can look very menacing, but they know the limits. Were you frightened?'

She is pale and still lightly moist. She is trying to assess the danger in a rational way.

'When I woke up I didn't know what was happening. I didn't know where I was. I just heard this terrifying noise and you were running out.'

'They scream and bark. They make a hell of a noise. I'm sorry you were frightened. But don't worry about them. This is Africa

102

and there are lots of them up on the mountain but, as I said, they almost never come down this far.'

Bertil has slept through it, and thank God that Lucinda isn't here to see the baboons. They are truly creatures of the dark side. I am anxious about how Nellie will take this incursion.

As we are having tea, Vanessa comes into the garden. She says she has a board ready for the morning, and wonders if I would ask Bertil if ten o'clock is good for him. Bertil appears, walking groggily, and she gives him the message herself. He is in his Vilebrequin cozzie and his hair is brushed in all directions; it's Harry Styles hair, so Nellie told me. She is up on teen fashion. Bertil's torso is white and a little soft, but a few weeks on a surfboard will put that right. For some reason I think that young boys should have muscles. It's my upbringing – the South African in me: England is peopled by a lardy variety of masculinity. And young women have become solid; they congregate on the street with other fat women to act out a kind of loud and improbable cheerfulness, which my cynical self believes is to compensate for the fact that men have detoured around them.

Vanessa says a whale has breached quite close to the beach. Does Bertil want to see it? Yes, he does. Nellie and I exchange smiles as they walk down through the garden. We are pathetically keen to see our children happy. I guess that the whale is mostly an excuse to get away from us. I envy them and I would like to see the whale if it hasn't already gone on its way to who-knows-where.

'What does "breached" mean?' Nellie asks.

'It just means that it has broken the surface of the sea, sometimes to blow, sometimes from *joie de vivre*.'

'Do whales have *joie de vivre*?'

'I believe so. God, I certainly hope so. If not they have wasted a lot of their time and mine with their leaping and frolicking in the sea for no purpose.'

We can see Vanessa and Bertil intermittently in the thick bushes as they walk down a path to the beach to look at the sea. There are always interesting things to say about the state of the sea and its moods and currents and waves. It is a sort of philosophical study in its own right.

Nellie says it's very promising that Bertil wants to learn to surf: since Lars and she separated, she has felt a huge responsibility for Bertil's happiness. I say that the anxiety never goes away, even when your children have grown up. I never expected that, even though I had heard it from many people. It's become a commonplace: parents never stop worrying. These beliefs swirl feverishly around the lives of the middle classes of London.

'Oh God, are you sure?' says Nellie.

'Yes, I am sure.'

I suffered great pain when Lucinda became an addict. I was advised to push her out of the house – even to throw her out of the house – and leave her to her own devices so that she could come to terms with her drug-taking. That was the psychiatrist's line. I didn't believe a word of it, but I was desperate to help Lucinda and I could think of no better way. It was the most difficult thing I have ever done, to take my only daughter's suitcase and her clothes and to throw them into the street. I felt like Abraham in the land of Moriah – making a sacrifice for a higher purpose. The tawdry, crushed and stained clothes in her suitcase were pitiful to me. She picked the case up and walked uncertainly down the road as though any direction would be as good as the next. I hoped that no one in Notting Hill had observed this forced exit and misunderstood my apparent cruelty. I lay on my bed, distraught, for hours. I didn't have the strength to move. I felt as if I had parted with my humanity. How had I been persuaded to do the thing I least wanted to? I was desperately anxious about where she was sleeping and where she was spending her days – perhaps with dealers – or what she was doing to buy food. I knew that dealers were everywhere. After six weeks I was so worried I decided to get her back, but I could not find her. She had slid deep into the junkie world. I hired a detective to look for her, so that he could tell me where she was and I could at least check up on her occasionally. He came up with nothing after three weeks. Nothing except the bill. He had no trouble locating that promptly, just before I fired him.

I was given a tip-off by one of her friends. It turned out that Lucinda had found a flat with some other troubled kids and there they made a life of a sort for a few months. It was a life dominated by the need to find money to buy heroin. I visited the flat and it was so chaotic and filthy and insanitary that it looked as though it was some kind of installation depicting the end of civilisation, with all the inmates drifting in and out of consciousness on the banks of the Lethe, the river of forgetfulness, now relocated in unlovely Peckham.

It took me a few weeks to extricate Lucinda. I tried to persuade her to have a crack at the clinic in California.

'Crack? Like a weird choice of words, Dad,' she said. 'Did you say crack?'

'Sorry,' I said, 'not a very good choice under the circumstances, no. I will come with you and live near by if it helps.'

We laughed at the idea. I was clutching at anything drifting on the stream. But in truth my heart was being sundered. She looked so vulnerable, clearly unable to live in this world, as if the drugs had inducted her into a realm without hope of redemption and without anything remotely rational as a guide. She had a butterfly tattooed on her neck, and on one nostril her nose was pierced in five places. The butterfly reminded me of the suicidal moths in my aunt's sitting room, her *sitkamer*. Worse, she had two silver bobbles side-by-side on her tongue – which I learned were called a venom piercing – and another right through the septum with two bobbles on either side. I wondered, fastidiously and absurdly, what happened if she needed to blow her nose. I was thinking back to childhood colds. Now I found it almost unbearable to look at her. When she was a child I changed nappies willingly and I wiped her face with a flannel and performed all the little intimacies of parenthood. I have always cherished the memory of those days of innocence. She would ask for me in these intimate moments, rather than Georgina or the nanny, and I was secretly pleased. There were many nannies who always had problems with Georgina.

As we talked, Lucinda's piercings caught the light intermittently; I was faced with a zombie, someone who could hardly speak a simple sentence without muttering and chanting. As a way through the miasma I tried to speak calmly to her about what piercing meant – as if meaning was relevant to this conversation. My words seemed to be hopelessly inadequate and trite. It was as though I was speaking a language that had gone extinct. She mumbled something about the venom piercing being the most powerful of her piercings. I assumed from this that piercing had a mystical importance. I have seen African men and women – Maasai and

106

Zulu – with round, decorated wooden plugs in the earlobes, and they seemed to be carrying on a beautiful practice, something interestingly folkloric; they weren't doing it as an advertisement of otherness. Or of delusion. It was difficult for me to understand the point of piercing in London: it appeared to me to be self-hating, a form of obsession, and I found that hard to bear. I tried to discover what this piercing indicated – I consulted young people awkwardly – but I also found it difficult to accept that totally irrational beliefs could have taken root in my beloved daughter and that a sort of rampant mycological growth was advancing blindly within her brain. Maybe something like that has infected Jaco too, although with a different kind of madness.

Finally, after four long months, Lucinda agreed to go to California and we set off for Marin County.

9

In the morning I get up early to go to the airport to fetch Lucinda. Nellie offered to come with me but I thought it might be better to go alone because I could not be sure what state of mind Lucinda would be in. I am apprehensive.

The airport has a down-home quality: rugby shirts, biltong, popular novels and crude souvenirs are on sale beside Xhosa beads and bracelets, knock-off Dogon figures, zebra-skin rugs, and diamonds. I once bought a diamond here as a last-minute offering for Georgina as I waited for a plane. She wore it attached to a thin gold chain. After a row she put it away, and I never saw it again.

African women in a uniform, which looks like a housecoat, walk about in small, sociable knots, their feet scraping the floor, as if indicating that they are not in a hurry. I have never understood what this foot-dragging signals –perhaps it's a kind of insouciant sexiness – but I remember it clearly from Tannie Marie's farm, all those years ago. All those years ago, when I was innocent.

In the hall I wait anxiously for the plane from San Francisco via Johannesburg to land. I can see the glassed-in passage in which Lucinda will appear. The plane is delayed. I call Nellie.

'We are quite happy, darling. Bertil and Vanessa are surfing, and kissing.'

'Did you see them?'

'They can't stop. It's so sweet. Adorable.'

'The plane is late. That's why I rang.'

'Okay, don't stress, we are very happy. I went in the sea. In a wetsuit, but still it was cold. My head was aching. In the Baltic the water is warm.'

'I know, it's all my fault. Also, allow me to take this opportunity to apologise that we don't have wild strawberries and lingonberries and trolls. And by the way, the Baltic is mostly fresh water. This water here comes all the way down from the northern Atlantic in deep currents and wells up just about in front of the house. Not like your little softy inland sea. Oh, okay, I hear now that the flight has landed and is taxiing to its berth. We should be home at about one for lunch. What is Lindi making?'

'She has made pickled fish. Is that nice?'

'Nice? Nice? It's epic. It's the finest thing you will ever eat, and it is totally delicious, and compulsory. It's Malay, very traditional. Not only that, but Lindi makes the best pickled fish in the whole of Cape Town – and suburbs. *Jag älskar dig*, Nellie.'

'I love you too. Keep working on the Swedish. You have a limited vocabulary, but a sexy accent.'

It takes some time for the first passengers to appear in knots, looking like a defeated army coming home exhausted and beaten. Even their luggage seems to have taken a battering. I see a small beagle checking baggage for drugs as the doors to customs open. I hope Lucinda isn't foolish enough to have brought drugs with her. The beagle looks diligent, and in love with its work. It wears a tabard just so we know what its vocation is: *Drug enforcement*.

I wait patiently; what's a few more minutes when you haven't seen your only child for so long? Before she went to California, she seemed to believe that taking drugs was a higher calling, something like the beagle's. She once went into a reception at the US Ambassador's house in Regent's Park with cocaine in a bag. An electronic sensor ran over her clutch bag; it signalled her guilt and she was taken to a small room, smiling vacantly and shrugging her shoulders to suggest that officious and unenlightened nobodies were making trouble at the behest of the ruling classes.

'It's a fit-up, people,' she said to innocent guests. I was mortified.

My connections to the Ambassador eventually prevailed over the law, and Lucinda was released. Her defence was infuriating: she said the rules were absurd and fascist. If she needed a little coke in the ladies' powder room, who was being harmed? I long ago discovered that taking drugs leads to a kind of irritating obduracy, as though the user is somehow blameless, and the rest of the world is blinkered. And yet my love for her is unconditional. Even in the course of our worst times, my frustration with her was inseparable from love. And even now my instinct is to console her at all times, whatever pain she has caused me.

The doors open and I catch sight of Lucinda. My heart is pounding and tumbling within my chest. She emerges with a mountain of luggage. She is holding the hand of a small child. A black child. How kind of her. She waves. She skips, and points at me for the benefit of the child. Why would you point out a stranger? And then I realise what is going on: this child is with Lucinda. Lucinda waves again and hurries to the barrier. I kiss her and she hugs me. The little boy holds on to her hand and retreats behind this laager of grown-ups.

'Daddy, how wonderful. It's so great to see you. It's like it's been years. Like for ever.'

She looks very good; her eyes are no longer scrunched up defensively and her face has filled out a little, so that I see once more my girl. My treacherous tears react. The memories of the struggle we have had, and the hell she has been through, well up inside me. I am only just suppressing my tears, which have a sort of autonomy, an independence from my rational self.

'Don't cry, Daddy. Look, this is Isaac, and he is coming along.'

'Is he yours, darling?'

I ask it as evenly as I can manage.

'He's the son of my boyfriend, Emerante, who is a musician from Haiti. His ex-partner decided she wasn't going to look after him while Emerante went to WOMAD. What could I do?'

I hardly understand what she is saying.

'Are you allowed to take this child with you?'

'No problem. He has a child passport and I used his mother's passport. I am more or less his mother anyway. She's white in case you were wondering.'

I take little Isaac up in my arms.

'Hello, little Isaac, my name is Frank.'

'Hello, Grandpa,' he says. 'Why are you crying?'

'Grandpa is pleased to see you, Isaac,' says Lucinda.

'Did you talk to him about me? How old is he?'

'He's two and six months. Yes, I told him all about you and what a wonderful father you have been and I told him you are his grandfather. I showed him pictures of you.'

I am a little disturbed by Lucinda's legerdemain with passports and grandfathers and genealogy.

Isaac is now holding my hand confidently. 'Hello, Grandpa,' he says.

'Hello, little Isaac.'

A porter loads up the mountains of luggage and wheels us to the parking garage. If you saw the luggage you might imagine that Marie Antoinette was travelling incognito. I wonder if I can call Nellie to tell her that Isaac is coming. I decide against it. We drive out of the airport and onto the main highway; I am once again ashamed of the shacks that line the road and the plastic bags which my mother so loathed flying across the highway in the wind, and I note the cattle and goats grazing on the verge – more like foraging hopefully for anything edible – and I note the small dead animals beside the road, cats and feral dogs. I feel as if I am personally required to explain these shacks and animal corpses to Lucinda and to put them into context – e.g., the exit from the rural areas, which leads me to a brief detour on the effects of liberation, and includes a short talk on the role our ancestor had in this history, a history which has led by winding and unpredictable routes to this misery and squalor.

We rush towards Table Mountain, holding the astounding, improbable mountain in our gaze through the windscreen so that the squalor on either side of the road is quickly forgotten. The mountain is misted in blue, like cigarette smoke. In some weathers it looks like a huge liner, moored to the flatlands we are now crossing. I say that it is a World Heritage Site and how as a boy at school we walked the paths and climbed up the gorges on Sundays. Sunday was the only day we were allowed out of school

112

and for me it was an escape to the heights and the deep shade and the streams of brownish water coursing down through the forests, and the ropes of climbing plants that reminded me so vividly of the Tarzan films I had seen. There were places up there where we would swim. I tell Lucinda about Jan Smuts, one-time Prime Minister, who loved the mountain and ensured that it would never be built on above a certain level, so that wherever you are in Cape Town you see the massive green and blue and purple mountain looming above. It is, I say, my cathedral.

'God, it is so beautiful,' says Lucinda. 'It's awesome.'

'It's awesome,' says Isaac cheerfully.

'Don't worry, he repeats everything.'

I can't call Nellie. But I am pretty sure she will rise to the occasion. She is Swedish for a purpose, to advance the cause of tolerance. We plunge down towards the Atlantic and my house, and Lucinda is again struck by the view, as though it were arranged just for her; she is a little proprietorial, as if all these natural wonders are the better for being viewed by her. When I point out some whales hugging the shore – the whales are busily heading north in numbers – she asks me to pull over so that she can study them, or perhaps so that she can share their insights. Whales are held in high esteem in California.

They are soon gone.

'The whales have gone, little Isaac.'

'Whales have gone,' says Isaac.

'They are going home.'

'Going home,' says Isaac.

We pull up at the house. Lindiwe is waiting for us, and Bertil emerges from his tower in his new life-saver's shorts, looking like a surf dude already; his shoulders and nose are a little burnt and his hair seems to have been bleached. Vanessa and he have been listening to music. Nellie hugs Lucinda. Lindiwe hugs her too.

'Who is this lovely little person?' Nellie asks.

Lindiwe, trying to be helpful, speaks to the little boy in Xhosa.

'He is the son of Lucinda's boyfriend,' I say. 'He is American.'

'His name is Isaac. His father is away at WOMAD,' says Lucinda, as if rock music has an indisputable precedence over all other forms of human endeavour.

'How gorgeous you are, Isaac,' says Nellie, picking him up. He puts his thumb in his mouth and strokes his own hair. His eyes seem to glaze over with contentment.

I wonder, as parents do, how my daughter could have neglected to give me such important news.

'When he has his thumb in his mouth, that means he is happy,' says Lucinda. Her smile is wonderful to me.

She turns to Bertil: 'I have heard so much about you from my father, Bertil. It's like great you could be here too.'

I am pleasantly surprised that Lucinda should be so tactful and sociable. Until recently there was only one topic of interest and that was her relationship to her karma; her karma, she said, was fragile as a result of her actions in previous states of existence. This was the sort of wisdom that she has picked up on the journey.

'Right, let's unpack and we will have lunch.'

Nellie shows them to their bedrooms; she decides that Isaac should sleep in Lucinda's room and she says we should hire a cot for him. Also, Nellie finds that Lucinda has not brought many baby clothes, so I offer to take a trip to Woolworths after lunch if she gives me a list. I also ask Lindiwe if she knows someone who could do some child-minding. Yes, she does. Her cousin will come any time she is required.

Bertil and Vanessa are sitting on the swing chair together.

'Are you staying for lunch, Vanessa? There is plenty.'

'Thanks, Mr McAllister, that would be great. I will just call my mom to tell her.'

She glances at Bertil. He looks down, smiling ambiguously, perhaps to mask a little discomfort.

Rock pigeons are calling and sunbirds are busy probing for nectar in the protea flowers. A chanting goshawk whistles somewhere up above and the neurotic guinea fowl are protesting; they have a restless mentality, a crowd mentality, always rushing, and suddenly stopping, and then milling about as if they are waiting for the next rabble-rouser to speak and sometimes they take flight, screaming without reason. All these calls are familiar and reassuring to me.

Over lunch Nellie sits with Lucinda; little Isaac is wedged between them. Nellie is enchanted by Isaac; he has a quality of warmth I have never before encountered in a very small child, a precocious empathy. He is the centre of attention, not because he is so young, not because he is being promoted in the self-serving way that parents affect, but because he is an innocent.

'Hello, Grandpa,' he says to me.

'I told him Dad was his grandpa,' Lucinda says to Nellie.

'Hello, to you, Isaac. What do you want to eat?'

'Cookies. And ice cream, Grandpa.'

'Is that okay, Lucinda?'

'Oh. Sure. He had a huge breakfast on the plane.'

I can't quite see the connection between breakfast and ice cream. Lindiwe brings a cone of vanilla ice cream. Isaac licks it carefully.

'Very cold,' he says.

We wait expectantly to hear his next judgement. And here we are, sitting in the shade, overlooking the sea, a very modern family, lulled by warmth and affection.

The afternoon is becoming hotter. The wind off the sea has died. We walk down to the beach and I dive in and body-surf on a few modest waves. Nellie walks with Isaac and Lucinda towards the huge rocks to the north where the boy was drowned some years ago. I run rather stiffly along the beach to catch up with them.

'Not bad, Dad,' says Lucinda. 'You look good. For ninety-seven, that is.'

'Ho, ho. Don't give up the day job.'

'Not bad, Grandpa,' says Isaac.

'Want a swim in the sea, big boy?'

'Yes please, Grandpa.'

We walk down to the water. I pick him up and we move slowly until his little feet are in the water. I lower him carefully so that he is lying in the water.

'Brrr ... cold,' he says, wriggling.

His hair is quite bushy, something like the coiffeur of the early Jackson Five. He is shivering as I dry him.

'I love you, Grandpa,' he says.

There are tears in my eyes again, fortunately indistinguishable from seawater.

As I set off for the Woolworths in the nearby fishing village, *a kind of joy comes over me*. For the moment I cannot remember the rest of the quote, hard as I try.

I love the drive down to the harbour and the village and the perfect bay beyond. It's a makeshift little town with a fish-processing factory near the harbour; the harbour is home to indolent breakaways from the seal colony about half a mile out to sea; the refusenik seals lie luxuriously on pontoons and on the harbour wall. Having forsaken the traditionally active life of the seal, which demands some vigorous swimming, they have opted for hand-outs. Occasionally they will bark; this bark lacks conviction.

A sprawl of suburban houses is gathered around the port and is climbing up the hills. Some of these houses are Spanish in their inspiration, others are thatched in rondavel style, others have cheap modernist leanings. All of them have elaborate electrified fences.

The main road to the harbour is sometimes covered with sand driven in by the wind. A huge sand hill has appeared where once there was a car park. Up on the hills some way from the port, a squatter camp has appeared in the last twenty years. The residents come from all over Africa. It is a violent place, known to the white locals as Mandela Park.

Woolworths has everything I can think of for little Isaac. I buy a collapsible cot, shorts, small sneakers, swimming trunks and a hat; also socks, underpants, a mound of nappies, a drinking beaker and a sou'wester, in case it should rain. I find some small denim dungarees, and I buy these too. The butcher has some of the finest *boerewors*, he says, and I take a few kilos to freeze. I buy a bunch of dill for Nellie. At the harbour shop I buy six live lobsters from a tank and some tuna steaks. The ready-cooked lobsters, lying on ice, have a deep red colour, the colour of arterial blood. I am in a frenzy of buying and providing as if I am expecting a long siege.

Back at the house Nellie and Lindiwe come out to help unload all I have bought.

'Where's Lucinda, darling?'

'Oh, she's a little tired, and so is Isaac. They are both soundly asleep. Do you say soundly asleep?'

'Sound. Sound asleep. But soundly is good.'

'Okay, sound. And Bertil and Vanessa are down on the beach.'

'I'll light the fire. I think I may have bought too much. I went slightly mad.'

'I see. But the more the better.'

'You know that a *braai* is a sacred rite here. It's like Sankta Lucia, with fire and meat. We take it very seriously. It makes us what we are.'

'What's that?'

'Candidates for a coronary. But we are having lobsters and tuna. I found some dill as you asked.'

'Great, I will make Swedish mayonnaise.'

Nellie chops dill to stir into her mayonnaise and Lindiwe, as usual, has anticipated what I want and she has stacked the wood neatly beside the *braai*. I feel uneasy about her devotion to me and my comforts, but it is hard to resist. I light the fire – men's work. In Africa some tribes still keep the sacred fire going at all times and I understand why: the smoke is a message to heaven, a reminder that we exist. Nobody wants to believe that they are adrift in an uncaring universe.

The idea is to boil the lobsters for a few minutes and then to grill them in the shell and to put the tuna on a lower heat to the side. I have no qualms about boiling lobsters and watching their last quadrille as their carapaces change from Byzantine blue to haematite, a mineral red. That is the moment when you take them out of the water.

Nellie and I sit down with a glass of sparkling wine as the fire comes to life.

'Did Lucinda give you any more explanation?'

'Of Isaac? Not really, she says she had no choice.'

'Do you mind having him?'

'Of course not. I am already in love with little Isaac.'

'You are right on trend. It's become fashionable among the whites here to adopt orphan children, often because the mother has died of AIDS.'

'Frank, it worries me, how did she manage to bring the child in?'

'Don't tell anybody, but she said that she borrowed her boyfriend's ex-partner's passport. I just hope there isn't some sort of hoopla when she goes. Here come the young lovers.'

We smile at Bertil and Vanessa encouragingly, as though they would benefit from our approval. The fact is, I am eager for their approval and affection. I have accepted that Nellie speaks to them more naturally than I do. She has a quality which young people quickly recognise: she is genuinely interested in them.

Bertil and Vanessa approach the fire, staring at the flames as though drawn, like moths. The wood is burning bright and giving off the scent of eucalyptus.

'How's the surfing going?' Nellie asks.

'We went to Muizenberg with Vanessa's brother, and we surfed there.'

'How did that go?'

Vanessa points at Bertil as though we need to locate him.

'Bertil can stand up on his board already. It's like amazing. Awesome. Natural talent.'

She makes a fist and bumps it against Bertil's knuckles. He laughs rather desperately and rolls his eyes.

Vanessa says, 'Respect, bru,' to Bertil, before giving him another fist bump.

I wonder if I should speak to Vanessa's mother about drugs. She paints the harbour and the mountains in acrylic and sells the pictures at the weekly market. Sometimes she paints pictures of the squatter camps, the corrugated-iron walls, the buckets of water carried by children, the blue doors and window frames on the shacks, children playing with old inner tubes and tyres, the occasional donkey pulling a cart, which has the axle and tyres of a small car. All these scenes are in demand from tourists. Vanessa's mother, Selina, wears wispy, trailing clothes, as if she is a postulant fairy; on reflection I don't think news of marijuana in Kent is going to worry her. As boys we used to smoke Swazi Gold or Durban Gold, the best in the world, we believed. We were always inclined to believe that South Africa was, in some way, world class. The best stuff grew wild in the mountains of Swaziland, a kind of Valhalla for hippies.

I wake Lucinda but leave little Isaac asleep. She groans and stretches and turns over.

'Food's up.'

'I am not hungry.'

'The lobsters are ready.'

'Oh, okay, give me a few minutes while I shower.'

'Okay.'

I see her mother's almond eyes as she appraises me for a moment.

I sit next to little Isaac, watching him breathe. I am hoping he will wake up soon, but he's out for the count. I am waiting eagerly for his *levée*. My mind is a little volatile. It ranges over Piet Retief's death to the sardine run which is due to arrive in the bay any day now. I have never seen it, but the locals say you can catch your supper in a hat. If you want to catch your supper in a hat. I wonder, too, if Cousin Jaco is safely back in the bosom of his church; I have a feeling I haven't seen the last of him.

I hear a muffled childish cry. Little Isaac is awake.

'Hello, Grandpa,' he says. His face appears to be soft and vulnerable, as though sleep has made it malleable.

'Hello, Isaac. Are you hungry?'

'I am, Grandpa.'

'Okay, I will just change your nappy.'

I feel blessed as I clean him up. He lies amongst the mess amiably.

'You have big ears, Grandpa.'

'Yes, I suppose I do. Compared with yours anyway.'

My ears do appear to be getting bigger; perhaps they are trying to keep pace with my face.

10

Nellie and I walk hand in hand along Muizenberg Beach, which stretches into the distance. Lucinda and Isaac are making a dam in the sand. As Nellie walks, she radiates contentment. Inevitably I compare her to Georgina, with her moods and resentments. Her every instinct was to be restless and discontent. There was no place or circumstance that did not agitate her, and often the implication was that I was somehow to blame for her agitation. I began to believe it myself.

Nellie is almost implausibly enthusiastic. She looks out to sea, where Bertil is learning to surf. I point her towards Seal Island, and she says it is beautiful. In the junction where the waves meet the mountain, they are regular and relatively easy to ride. Sometimes great white sharks are spotted cruising with menace in the surf. But today there is no shark warning outside the surf shop – a red flag bearing an outline of a shark – and I doubt if Bertil will anyway get far enough into the water to be at risk. When we left him with Vanessa and the coach, he was standing on a board in the shallows. The surfing coach is a former world champion, Vanessa says. The reverence for sporting success is strong here; it is a substitute for thinking the unthinkable about the future. The coach has a distinct paunch under his wetsuit.

The beach stretches for twenty miles towards the Hottentot Holland Mountains to the east. I see myself as holding stock in all this sky and beach and mountains. This endless beach has always been democratic, open to all, despite the efforts of the apartheid government to segregate it.

A fishing boat has come ashore and is being pulled up the sand; two of the crew are hauling in the nets. I wave to Lucinda and Isaac to come see. A small crowd of people wait to find out what is in the nets. The coloured women are ready with their enamel basins. Little Isaac is very excited. He laughs when the fish wriggle.

The fish are red roman, stumpnose, and some steenbras; they are all familiar to me. I buy a whole stumpnose for the barbecue. I exchange pleasantries with the fishermen, showing off a little, always keen to speak Afrikaans. There are nuances in Afrikaans, which I value. I tell Nellie that these coloured people are not happy with the advance of the Xhosa squatters from the Eastern Cape, who live along the edge of the coast road in shacks in the bush. I say that the coloured people believe they have been marginalised by the African government; nothing has changed for them.

An older fisherman addresses me as 'Master', which makes me uneasy. He asks for a cigarette, but I don't smoke. He can hardly believe it. He shakes his head as if to say the world has gone to pot. His face has weathered so that every wrinkle seems to be neatly folded onto another, like linen panelling in a Tudor house. His few remaining teeth are yellow, and his eyes are watery and filmed over. Perhaps tens of years out in the glare on this bay have damaged his eyes. They appear to be weak and barely focused, like a kitten's.

The fisherman says that white stumpnose are declining in numbers, and that is why my fish is expensive. He seems surprised that I should have been willing to spend so much money. The white stumpnose has a complacent demeanour, like a well-fed Greek Orthodox priest.

I am content, as if this landscape and these people are there for my happiness. Both speak to me. I take the fish back to the car and put it in a cool bag. I run rather clumsily over the deep sand, wishing I were bounding along, lithe and unbowed, as once I was. Further up the beach, in front of the surf shop, Vanessa is on her board and surfing with Bertil. They are both in very high spirits. Bertil gives us a wave, and they surf in for about twenty yards, before Bertil's board dips down and he falls head first into a wave. Vanessa glides up to him and holds his board in line while he climbs on again.

'They are having a great time,' says Nellie. 'It's wonderful to see him so happy.'

'It's pretty difficult not to be happy here.'

'I can see that.'

'I just hope that Lucinda is going to be reasonable.'

'Don't worry. We will look after her. She's been just fine so far.'

She doesn't want to usurp my parental role, but actually I think she will be better for Lucinda than I will. There is a kind of obduracy in Lucinda that quickly upsets me. And she can be pointlessly insistent at times.

'I am not sure if she will ever be right,' I say.

'Right?'

'Right in the sense that she may never recover from what happened with Georgina and then the drugs. I was reading only the other day that marijuana, never mind the hard drugs, warps and changes your brain for ever. She was such a sweet child. Nellie, what we did to her was inexcusable.'

'Don't be pessimistic. We will do our best. Please don't worry too much. She's a lovely girl.'

There is no hint of a reproach. Nellie has a touching inclination to look for the best qualities in everyone. I am keen to acquire this talent; I have always been too ready to judge. I put my arm around her and we stroll along the beach.

'What you did wrong,' Nellie says, 'is to marry the wrong person.'

'How do I find the right person?'

'Ah, that's up to you. Of course. I could not possibly give you any clues.'

She pronounces 'clues' as 'cloos'.

'No, I can see that would be wrong.'

'Also, we *skogsfru* come from the forest. A *skogsfru* lures men down into endless caves. No man can resist her seductive powers.'

'Goodness. Are you a fully paid-up *skogsfru*?'

'I might be.'

'Help, I may not be able to resist your charms.'

I start to run down the beach, bounding over kelp and streams. I slow down quite soon and in those few charged moments I see that we will be married. I have been rescued from bitterness and purged of resentment and I have found tranquillity with Nellie. I must marry her.

She is laughing when I come back at a gentle jog, panting.

'You can't run away from a *skogsfru*.'

'I can see that. If that's impossible, we might as well get married. Where would you like to be married?'

'Are you sure?'

'Of course. Where do you want to be married?'

125

'If you are serious, maybe here, maybe Sweden. I'm easy.'

'You know that "easy" also means promiscuous?'

'We Swedish women are famous for being promiscuous. It's not true, but the myth makes us seem more interesting than we really are.'

After a few minutes she says, 'Can we have a party in Sweden also? For my friends and relatives?'

She leads me into the water. She puts her arms around me. We are standing waist deep in the water. A thick rope of kelp brushes against my leg and for a moment I think I have trodden on a sand shark. A wave knocks us over. We disappear for a few seconds under a wave.

Isaac is crying when we come out of the water. He is confused and upset, even though Lucinda has told him we were just swimming. I pick him up. His curly hair brushes my face as he hugs me. He puts his thumb in his mouth for a moment.

'Did you swim, Grandpa? Can I swim, Grandpa?'

I take him waist deep and pretend to dunk him. He laughs wildly, as though it is the most wonderful thing he has ever known. Nellie towels him off. We go on to the ice-cream shop which sells rum-and-raisin and chocolate and tutti-frutti ice creams as well as plain vanilla. That's their full range and I take pleasure in buying everyone an ice cream, especially one that evokes my childhood. Nellie suggests we stop at the sports shop to buy Isaac a small wetsuit. I buy one for Bertil too.

'That's, that's so cool,' he says.

The mountain behind is a deep, deep green, broken by the leaves of the silver trees, which are more gun-metal grey than silver. On a walk with school friends on this mountain – we were

126

about thirteen – we were attacked by coloured boys, some of them possibly living on the mountain, *bergies* – who pelted us with large stones so that we had to run back to Boyes Drive. I was in fear of my life.

Now we take the high-level Boyes Drive and descend to a café further along the coast; it has fine coffee and a pleasantly louche atmosphere. The plates and teacups are all different as if acquired in house sales. It's just the sort of place Georgina would have hated.

When we reach home the sun is going down directly off-shore. It moves fast; you can see it moving as it is pared away by the horizon and then quickly dragged into the sea. But the sky beyond is magnificent; from below the horizon, the sun is colouring listless clouds in pink and gold and Naples yellow.

I prepare the barbecue happily, using wood I bought from squatters along the road, neatly sawn and tied into bundles. They told me they were refugees from the Congo. I spoke to them in French.

'*C'est une vie dure,*' they said.

'*Oui, je le crois.*'

And I can easily imagine that life is hard in the Congo; it is one of those countries we believe is always on the brink of anarchy. I blame Joseph Conrad.

The two men said that the locals hated them.

A whole stumpnose requires delicate treatment, wrapped in foil, before direct exposure to the wood embers. Nellie cleans and scales the fish; she says that Swedes know how to do this kind of thing; they are close to nature. She offers to make a salsa verde. Lindiwe wants to know how it is done. The barbecue is under a white milkwood tree, out of the wind, and I have a table fashioned from a long slab of Table Mountain granite. The massif of the mountain above and behind us is made of granite and sandstone.

'Am I embarrassing you by saying I love you?' Nellie asks.

'Of course not. Say it as often as you can. I am amazed that you love me, but I can't have enough of it.'

I hug her; she is richly perfumed by basil and mint and garlic.

'You smell fragrant. That's enough for me. I am marrying salsa verde. Nellie, honestly, I have never been so happy.'

And it's true. I wonder why I have taken so long to acknowledge that I was deeply unhappy with Georgina.

The children appear from the beach. I guess that they have been kissing. They stop holding hands. Bertil looks a little flustered, in case we should see the rash of passion on their avid mouths. You don't want to expose young love to your parents. Young love is anyway transient, a summer storm.

The stumpnose is wonderful. The salsa is perfect. The fire is glowing bright now, holding the darkness at bay.

II

An unwelcome email from Jaco arrives:

Oom Frank, I am maybe going be in a documentry about my time in Scientology. A journalis from the BBC have phoned me. He says all I must do is tell him my story. I had a crash what they call a wreck in the US because the traffic lights doesn't change like they say it will when I have become a Clear. They says I must pay them back for the other guy's car because he was on green. They say I owe them $5,000 for the insurance. Oom jy moet my glo, dit is kak. Die hele ding is kak. Dit het absoluut niks omdien Die Here to doen nie. Oom, it is all shit, it's just to make money. It has fuck all to do with God. It's not a fucking church at all, just a bunch of mad people what believes you can fly to Mars by will power. When I ask them how you are supposed to breathe on this journey they says I have disrespected the founder Elron Hubbard. I have tried to speak to Tom Cruise because he is a nice guy but he says he does not take part in management decisions. He is walking to the tennis court for his coaching and he have no time to stop. I was sweeping leafs. I put my hand on his arm and one of the ouks with him pushes me away so I give him a broken nose and blood is pouring out and I run that night because I know I must find a way to phone you, Oom. I thank you and God for getting me out. A few days ago I speak with this journalis he phoned me again from London and *he says he is filming a doccumentry about these people and he wants me to tell my story. I am living in Potch temporarally on the farm now but I want to take your advice on if I shall do this doccumentry. Like I say this journalist wants me to go to London to speak about what happened to me. He says the BBC will pay the flight. Maybe I can sell my story but you have to be careful with these people. I tried to bell your cell phone but it is not working. I want to speak with you urgently, Oom, please. Please bell me.*

Alles van die beste, Jou neef Jaco

Jaco leaves his telephone number. I don't reply. I have a strong feeling that he is trouble. He doesn't know I am in Cape Town, and I don't want a visit from him.

12

I have hired a lodge for a few days at a reserve on the sea near the Tsitsikamma Forest. It's about three hours east from my house and we are heading there for a weekend so that Nellie can see something of the country and some wild animals; in fact, so that we can all see the wonders I have been talking up. I have planned the journey to include a detour through the wine lands. My grandfather owned one of the great estates many years ago. We plan to stop at Franschhoek, a beautiful small town where we will have lunch on the veranda – the *stoep* as we like to call it – of my favourite restaurant, Le Quartier Français.

As we descend from Hells Hoogte – Hell's Heights – I feel as though we are crossing the border to a secret but familiar and blessed world, a series of valleys and steep passes to wild mountains which suggest all kinds of possibilities, which include small towns that have hardly changed in a hundred and fifty years. But I know that this intimacy with the landscape is self-serving, a pleasant delusion. We drive down through the valley with vines on both sides of a road that follows the valley floor to Franschhoek, where we have lunch on the *stoep* and set off again somewhat reluctantly to drive up and over the pass. The last elephant was seen leaving the valley in the nineteenth century on this pass, just about the same time my ancestor left a nearby valley for his own Eden, where he was killed.

Bertil is a little quiet, perhaps wishing he could have stayed with Vanessa, but he has his new surfboard strapped to the roof. After all, Vanessa has said that he is a natural and there are plenty of beaches where we are headed. Also, there are deep forests, where one wild elephant cow lives on, all alone, the last survivor of a great herd that had been there long before the white people arrived with their guns. It's a sad story. When I was young I knew a girl who went for a walk in the forest on her own and was never seen again. At that time there were thought to be thirteen elephants living in the forest, and they were known to be very aggressive.

You could see this country as a kind of tapestry, intimately woven of beautiful landscapes and violent death. Some of the whites say that it is stimulating. At least it's never dull here, they say.

The drive into the reserve is beguiling. When we open the windows of the car we can hear the roaring of the sea in the distance. On the dirt road towards the lodges, we see three tortoises and two snakes. We slow to a halt so we can look at the snakes closely. One is unmistakably a puff adder and the other a grass snake, I think. It's certainly green. Lucinda is frightened, but the snakes are inert although their ever-alert tongues are testing the air. Bertil wants to know if they are poisonous. I tell him that the puff adder kills more people than any other snake, because it does not move fast and strikes when anyone comes too close. It lies on the road, full of truculent menace. In the background male ostriches, in their dandyish fashion, are displaying – unleashing their wings and dancing with a vain dipping movement designed to impress a drab female ostrich.

Further in the distance there are some Hartmann's zebras, the mountain zebra that not long ago was almost extinct. We are against animals and plants becoming extinct. We have adopted these politically neutral causes because we lack a moral or political role.

Our lodge overlooks a lagoon at the point where a beer-coloured river runs into it. The sea is rushing urgently through a gap in the sand bar into the lagoon. The lagoon and the river are home to otters. The guide notes say these are the Cape clawless otter. The notes also promise fish eagles. As we approach our lodge, we see a group of antelope, *bontebok*. They are dark and brown-and-white in patches, each patch sharply differentiated, as if they are maps of contiguous countries. They have white faces and horns shaped like a lyre. Their tails switching, they glance at us without interest before going back to grazing. As we are unloading we hear the forlorn, haunting cry of the fish eagle. It rips violently and ecstatically through the more gentle background chorus of the cicadas and the small birds and the base of the distant pounding of the waves. Some African tribes believe the cry of the fish eagle is a protest of the dead from beyond the grave.

Isaac and Nellie and Bertil and I go for a walk. Lucinda says she is still jet-lagged and needs a short sleep. She says that when she wakes up she will cook the leg of lamb we brought for supper. It is news to me that she can cook. I offer her a cookbook. She strokes my cheek and it warms to her touch.

'Are you enjoying yourself, Bertil?' I ask.

'It's great. It's really great.'

'I am enjoying myself, Grandma,' says Isaac.

I see that Nellie is moved: little, mysterious, affable Isaac is touching both of us. His presence confers undeserved credibility on us.

'I am so glad you are happy, Isaac.'

Nellie holds Isaac's hand, and he walks gamely on. After a while I offer to carry him on my shoulders, and he agrees, which pleases me. He says, 'Go horsey.'

Nellie, like me, wonders what the full story of Isaac is. Has his mother abandoned him – along with her passport – or has Lucinda appropriated the child? And are we complicit in some way? I will have to talk to Lucinda eventually. But now I feel a familiar resentment. Why has Lucinda taken this child? We can't spend weeks with an unknown child. We don't even know how long Lucinda is proposing to stay. My questions are treated lightly.

'Chill,' she says when I ask, 'let's just chill.'

Of course it is not that simple. She has a tendency to gloss over detail. I am aware that my disappointment springs from unrequited love; somehow I am expecting the perfect resolution for my daughter and I would also welcome some gratitude for my steadfastness in support. But with Lucinda, there is still the fear of imminent betrayal lurking in her mind. It may be the effect of drugs, a sort of persistent paranoia.

Now Bertil is carrying Isaac, who is acting as a lookout. He laughs uproariously and points when he sees more ostriches; they are in a mating frenzy everywhere, rushing here and there distractedly. We stop at a pristine beach above the bay where, we have been told, whales calve at this time of year. Just below us we see a mother leading her white calf towards the open sea. The males are white at birth. They are half underwater, breaching and blowing every so often. It is a poignant sight, these huge mammals setting

134

off to swim determinedly for thousands of miles back to their icy northern waters. I feel this migration is a test, as if the whales are in peril as they embark on their epic journey. Another whale follows, leading a calf to the turbulent ocean. Are the mothers nervous? Are they thinking about what could go wrong? I don't believe they are. A friend of mine who makes documentaries believes that there is a connection between us and other species to be explored. Whales have been candidates for an exchange of ideas between the species for some time. But still, I think that the bumper sticker which reads *What has a whale ever done for me?* contains a certain cynical truth.

When we get back to the lodge, Lucinda is roasting the promised leg of lamb on the barbecue, cookbook open. She seems to be very calm. Her smile reminds me of the happy child she once was. She hugs Isaac. She hugs me. She hugs Bertil and Nellie. She is wearing very short shorts, with a green T-shirt embossed with the words *Oakland Athletics*. Now that her face is no longer painfully ravaged and furtive, she's beautiful, like her mother.

'You seem to be happy, darling. How's it going?'

'Admit it, you're thinking "unnaturally wired", aren't you? No, I haven't taken anything is the answer. What's not to like here? By the way, a huge antelope came wandering by. Humungous animal with curly antlers and a bit of a straggly beard on its neck, like the Amish.'

'That's a kudu, for sure.'

'Are they dangerous?'

'Only in the mating season.'

'Oh, watch out, everybody, Daddy's getting a little risqué.'

And now we are settling down, each happy to play the role we have been given. I am especially happy to be teased by my daughter.

After supper, in the last of the light, Lucinda and I walk the short distance down to the lagoon.

'We must be back before it gets too dark.'

'Okay.'

'The lamb was wonderful, sweet pea. Perfect.'

'Thank you. I am not completely useless.'

She takes my hand.

'How is Mum?' she asks. 'Have you spoken to her recently?'

'Only when she calls about something she thinks is important. You know that the baby is due any day?'

'Yes.'

'Are you okay with that?'

'No, I am not okay with it at all. I find it disgusting. It's like it's all about her. It always was. She doesn't give a rat's arse about the baby. And this baby will be my sister, or brother, of a sort.'

She is suddenly upset. I hold her close.

'We'll be fine, sweetheart.'

'Sorry, Daddy, I just remember how she ignored me and put me down all the time so that I was scared to speak and how she hated children and then left us, and now she's having a baby at the age of forty-six. It's sick. And the whole business is aimed at us.'

'I am not sure that's totally true.'

I could add to her litany with my own grievances, but I restrain myself.

'It is true. Absolutely. And tacky.'

'Maybe. More at me than you.'

The sea in the mouth of the lagoon is moaning as the tide storms out. The sea itself is calm in the last of the light. The late glimmers of the sun create a symmetrical pattern on the water, a web of fish-scale reflections.

'You wouldn't be surprised if a mermaid surfaced,' I say.

'You old softie.'

Lucinda kisses me; she knows the reference, a mermaid book I had given her when she was six. She loved and cherished it. I ordered the essential prop, the detachable mermaid tail, but it was difficult to attach and seemed likely to lead to a drowning in our pool.

'Daddy, I am so glad you have hooked up with Nellie. She is good for you. Actually, she's good for all of us.'

In the night I wake to the sound of the waves in the mouth of the lagoon. Their mood has changed: they boom like distant canon fire.

'You are awake,' Nellie says.

'Yes. I can't help noticing that you are too.'

'Are you okay? You were sighing in your sleep.'

'I'm fine. I have disturbing dreams these days.'

'I know you do, *älskling*. But are you happy?'

Her face is lit by the moonlight coming through the window. Her cheekbones are high and her forehead is shiny, almost nacreous, as though she is the Lucia Queen of the island of Grinda and the light from the candles in her crown is falling exclusively on her.

'Nellie, I am fantastically happy. It's wonderful to have us all together. The best thing I can think of.'

137

'Lucinda told me that she hasn't felt this happy for two years.'

As she turns to me, her large eyes are caught for a moment by the light.

'Did she really say that? That's great. She looks so much better.'

What Lucinda says to Nellie is not always the same as what she says to me. She is more straightforward with Nellie, so I am encouraged.

Nellie hugs me, her body fitting with mine neatly like the Matisse cut-outs we saw in the exhibition at the Tate Modern. There are certain things middle-class people are obliged to do, and seeing the Matisse was one of them that year. Nellie, typically, was entranced by the accompanying film of the old man's unerring dexterity. There are a few people in this world at any one time who can do wonderful, even miraculous, things. I see these people as the shamans or prophets of our times. They are attuned to other modes and other concerns; in our restrained and circumscribed lives we look to them for the deeper truths. Not the advertised truths of religions or crackpot sects, but the works and the ideas that singular people produce, which enable a kind of transcendence to exist on this earth.

Near the most southerly tip of Africa, and encouraged by a restless lagoon, I think we are close to transcendence. I feel a distinct current running in Nellie's body. I remember the telegraph poles and the thrumming of the attached wires on the road that led to the old farm. I wondered then how these wires carried messages. Even now I don't really know. The messages, however terse, always contained something of importance, something urgent or tragic or congratulatory. After my mother died, my father never failed to send me a birthday telegram and a postal order to my boarding school. All gone.

Nellie holds on to me; her hold is light, ethereal. I am charged with a sense of the possible. Outside we hear briefly the night warning of a leopard – the sound of linen being torn – but we are safe in our lodge. Safe and content.

Et in Arcadia ego.

We know its secondary meaning and its terrible ambiguity: death is present in Arcadia. Some art historians say that all art derives ultimately from the appalling awareness of mortality. I believe that all religions are a response to mortality.

Nellie is asleep. I find myself worrying about Jaco and his troubles. I am searching my mind to see if there is some nuance I have missed. I will speak to Jaco tomorrow. If he goes public on the Scientologists he is opening himself to a fresh kind of hell.

13

What gets on Jaco's tits most about Potchefstroom these days is the black people. *Swart mense*. He does not like the way they walk around as though they own the place even though the town was founded by Voortrekkers in 1838 just after Piet Retief was murdered by the Zulus.

Everything here have been built by white people, by us. Black people has done fuck all. When the Boers arrives here the blacks is sitting on their arses watching a few cows wandering around. These people can spend hours looking at cattle although they haven't got a fucking clue how to fix them if they is sick. Sometimes they blow smoke up their noses. Many of the black kids was used to die very young. Now because of modern medicine they are breeding like flies. What for? I want to know. What is the use? They worse educated now than they was under apartheid. Apartheid was not so bad as what everyone says, ask a black, many of them says they was better off before. Now their own people is robbing them blind. It's a shame. The ANC crooks who runs the place is so fucking corrupt they is bleeding their own people to death. The blacks knows where they stand when the whites was in charge. There was respect. Now it's fucking chaos with murders, hijacking and fuck knows what all.

One good thing I have bought a gun with the money Oom Frank gave me but even that is a hassle. I must take a test and I must have a permit. More worser than that I must have two hours of instruction from a kaffer policeman who can't hit a watermelon with a shotgun from five metres away. I want to tell this fat *poes* so-called policeman that I am shooting since I am five and I don't need any help from a policeman straight from the bush, thank you. Also I have to write my ethnicity on the form. Why? I thought we was all equal now. Maybe they don't want too many whities buying guns but I keep my mouth shut. You have to. Now you can't even shoot on your own farm without a permit but no worries the black people can come and snare your buck at night or steal your sheep and the police does zip. Or they steal. The black people steal anything they can. They kill our cattle out on the veld and cut it up right there and sell it to butchers and they just jack up your *bakkie* on bricks and take the wheels. And God help you if you leave your radio in a car for two minutes, it goes like shit off a shovel. Democratic shopping. And another thing is getting me the hell in: my cousin hasn't answered me. He's too fucking important, he's turned into a sort of *Engelsman* with a medal from the British government for his success in business. If you ask me, he got the medal for giving money to politicians more like licking their arse. He's a *ware piepiejoller*. He's a Member of the British fucking Empire. When I go to England to play rugby ten twelve years ago the place was so cold and grey and shit I couldn't stand it. The whole fucking country is more or less the size of a sheep farm in the Karoo anyway. Still they call themselves an empire, how do you like that. And now my cousin who is also a Retief on his mother's side is so up his own arse you will think he was born in Buckingham Palace, not Jo'burg. Jewburg. You can't even say that no more. Oom Frank's dad was a commie also. Even Oom Frank hisself is really a commie deep down. He visited Thabo Mbeki and Oliver Tambo up in Lusaka with other big cheeses. It was in the papers the *Citizen* which was a pile of shit.

Jaco is sitting in a pub with Jannie and Stoffel.

He sends his cousin another email. It starts *Please Oom*. But Oom Poes MBE is busy or he has blocked his emails.

Potch has gone to hell. The streets is dirty, the university what was built by Afrikaners for religious reasons is now full of blacks. They eat their free lunch at the cafeteria and fuck off immediately. One or two writes papers, Ph.Ds, total crap nobody knows what they is about not even the blacks who writes them. They piss just about anywhere and they drop all their rubbish straight onto the street. They cut branches from the municipal gardens for firewood even jacarandas so the botanical gardens looks like a bomb fell on them. Sometimes they have *kak* art shows there what nobody likes but they look at masks and Bushman painting and shit rugs which is made from potato sacks and then their faces looks like they has a mealie up their arses as they are trying to say something which shows they are trendy. Or tries to pretend they knows what this bullshit means.

Jaco's phone rings. A researcher from Cape FM Radio tells him that a great white has eaten someone in Fish Hoek, Cape Town. The researcher says that there will be a debate about whether these sharks should be shot or tagged if they are seen near the bathing areas. They want Jaco to come down to Cape Town for the big debate on Cape FM Radio. As it happens Jaco would love to shoot a great white, the more the merrier in fact. It's them or us, take your pick. It's fine for these tree-hugger *poephols* to say the great whites must be protected. Great whites are bastards and he should

142

know he's been inches away from death. The researcher says, 'That's interesting, but please don't come on quite so gung-ho.'

Jaco has no idea what she means. He agrees to go – there's a fee and a plane ticket. He is in the Bourbon Street Pub, where he and some of his mates meet most days at lunchtime; he pays up, he's only had four Windhoeks, maybe five, and one dop of Commando brandy, who's counting. He leaves a message for Flip Steenkamp on his phone to tell him he's off to Cape Town.

'*Jammer ou maat ek moes Kaapstad – toe gaan vir die radio en televisie oukies.*' I must go to Cape Town for the radio and television people.

Cape FM. He hasn't been on that for a while, not since he came back from the States. Meanwhile four or five people has been killed by great whites and he has not had one call. Not one. Nitzs.

It's eleven o'clock. He climbs a little unsteadily into a *bakkie* they lend him and drives out to the farm to pack. His mood is completely changed. He sings 'Ring Of Fire'. He wishes he could sing good. Johnny Cash is his favourite singer, you can't beat him. He's so happy he even offers two black women a lift in the back of the *bakkie*. He never gives the black men a ride if he don't know them.

As he turns off onto the dirt road to the farm his phone rings again. Shit, it's Cousin Frank. He pulls over.

'*Ja, Oom*, thanks for calling.'

'Listen, Jaco, I am off to the Addo Elephant Reserve with my family. So I can't meet you now but I can speak on the phone. Maybe in a couple of days when we are in town.'

'No, that's only fine because I am op pad to Jo'burg to get the plane now right this minute. I am going to talk about sharks for Cape FM.'

'Okay, well I won't be able to see you at the house as I have my daughter here and so on. We will be back in Cape Town in a few days. You know Lucinda was in rehab and she must have peace and quiet? So when I am back I will call you and we can meet somewhere to talk. Basically I don't think you should do it. By the way I think your shark days may be a diminishing asset.'

Jaco has no idea what a diminishing asset is but he guesses it is not good.

'Thanks very much, Oom, *baie dankie, hoor*. Thank you. I am very grateful for all what you has done for me. And we will talk about the other *dinges*.'

'That's fine. But don't ask me for more money because I won't give it to you. And listen, whatever you do, don't say yes to the Scientology business until we have spoken.'

'*Ek verstaan, Oom,*' he says in Afrikaans to demonstrate his sincerity. 'I understand.'

'Jaco, *nog 'n ding*, did they put up the gravestone for Tannie Marie?'

'*Ja*, they did that. It looks great. Beautiful job. Just by the chickens' house.'

'She was good to me. Okay. Got to go.'

Jaco feels his anger rising. Why does my cousin think I will make trouble at his place disturbing Lucinda? What is a fruitcake as far as I know. And was I asking for money? No I was not, even though I am a little short. His cousin paid a lot for a gravestone, nearly a hundred thousand. Fuck all to Jaco. All his dosh is from England: a hundred grand is nothing to him, the rand is up to shit. What about giving something to those who are not under the earth?

At the farm Jaco bursts through the fly screen and hastily packs some clothes in an old suitcase. None of the family, thank God, is at home. They don't like me. They want me to fuck off. I'll show them.

A maid makes him a flask of tea and gives him something to eat for the journey. Her name is Hester. He fucked her once or twice when he was drunk, but we don't talk about that. He thinks she can still be in love with him.

Now she gives him *boerebiskuite*, which is rusks. He hates them. In California he liked cheesecake. Jewish cake. Still, very tasty … No question, Jews knows how to make money and cake.

14

My call to Jaco, intended to deter him and, from a safe distance, to advise him, has now had unwanted consequences: Jaco will be in Cape Town. I should have said I was in Brazil, or New York. My phone rings as I am sitting on the veranda watching some zebra coming down to drink. They have an unusual brownish tinge to their formal stripes. It's Jaco.

'Can't hear you. Very poor reception here, Jaco.'

I turn the phone off and activate call blocking. Jaco is like a dog that comes and buries its nose in your lap, or tries to hump your leg. (Maybe I, too, am reverting to the archetype – crude and insensitive.)

Little Isaac, Nellie and Bertil appear over the sand hills. I have insisted that they walk with a guide. Nellie waves. Isaac waves and runs gamely after Bertil down to the lodge. His hair is like a halo. I pick him up. The guide hangs back, so as not to intrude on this moment.

'Hello, Grandpa.'

'Hello, little Isaac. Did you see anything interesting?'

'We saw whales, Grandpa.'

'That's great. Would you like some cookies and juice?'

'Yes please, Grandpa.'

I go to the kitchen, holding his hand.

'These are Marie biscuits – cookies – Isaac, or you could have Baumann's Lemon Creams, which are my favourite.'

'Can I have Lemon Creams, like you, Grandpa?'

'Of course you can. And here's your juice. It's red grape juice.'

'Umm, lover-ly. Awesome.'

He slurps strongly on the straw, his cheeks hollowing. Nellie watches him, a devotee.

The guide is called Blikke. I invite him to have tea with us, but he will only stand at the edge of the deck. He takes five spoons of sugar in his tea. He also accepts a few Lemon Creams.

He checks if we have enough firewood and he offers to bring some fresh fish tomorrow. I ask him what he has. He can get *galjoen*, which means galleon. Yes please. It has a resemblance to a galleon under sail. Blikke can also get lobster from local fishermen. I order two. He says he will put them in the kitchen early in the morning in a coolbox.

He walks off into the distance. He carries a carved stick and he has bottled water in a rucksack in case we should be thirsty. I wonder if he enjoys his work. Nellie says he is incredibly knowledgeable; he knows every bird and every plant. He showed us some leopard tracks, she says. There are three leopards in the area at the moment, but they are solitary and very shy. He's only seen them twice. One may be pregnant; the tracks show that it has been mating with a big male. Blikke is hoping for cubs. It seems Nellie wants leopard cubs too, to regenerate the natural world. She says that numbers are rising fast, and they are now able to sell once-threatened animals like mountain zebra to private game reserves and to other national parks.

Bertil has changed subtly in the last few days; he is more relaxed and also unexpectedly witty. He has taken to this place, the unfamiliar birdsong, the mountain behind the house that pours cloud down its sides like cream running off a *tarte Tatin*, the crashing waves on the beaches. The air too is liberating and congratulatory.

He spends a lot of time talking to Vanessa on his phone, but not obtrusively. He passes on her good wishes. Vanessa, he says, saw a lot of whales just below the house. He asks me where they are headed and I say that they migrate to the far north and come back in April for five or six months to mate and calve. They only have one calf every two years. They are the second biggest whales on the planet.

We are all being drawn in to this fairy story; it is essentially a tale of a more innocent time. In a way we have the same longings as my ancestor Piet Retief had when he set out looking for his own Eden on the other side of the wild mountains. His joy at looking down in imperial fashion from his horse onto Zululand was his epiphany – and also one of his last days on this earth.

I tell Nellie about Jaco's call; she thinks I should avoid him: I've done my bit and after all we are on holiday. I agree, but deep down I believe that blood is thicker than water. In the morning we are off to see the Elephant Reserve, staying two nights. We are all looking forward to seeing the elephants. Like whales, they have qualities we should take on board. Lucinda seems to be utterly content as if she has been enrolled into a more soothing world, one that puts you directly in touch with the elemental.

My secretary, Liz, calls me. Should she send a scan of a letter from Georgina, she asks, in which Georgina accuses me of being the father of her forthcoming child? I ask Liz how wild and mad it is. Pretty bad: apparently I insisted on adding my semen to the mix. No, I don't want to read it. Just send it on to the lawyers.

This is the sort of behaviour that almost unhinged me towards the end of our marriage. Now I am more or less immune to her accusations. Maybe her latest accusation is evidence of a truly paranoid personality disorder. At times I wondered how I could have created such disturbance in Georgina's mind. Or if I am guilty of disturbing her mind. Now I don't want to hear a single word from her and I particularly don't want to think about her baby, however it is to be brought about. Yet, strangely, I remember fondly the scents that accompanied her and I can recall an image of her when she was young, her thick blonde hair tied in a loose twist and her breasts almost escaping from a cheesecloth blouse. But I am recalling an entirely different person. I remember that I bought the blouse for her on the King's Road for her twenty-second birthday. These places had passed their heyday, but they still offered more than clothes; they suggested that they were selling an enticing, carefree philosophy. In every song that filled the shops, there were subtexts – and in every book and magazine you read, there was a promise of a better world.

Liz also sends me the copy of William Wood's diary that I asked her to trace. I can't wait to read it. William was a remarkable boy. Liz has found more, an account of what happened to him after he sailed away from Port Natal. He is thought to have gone to Brazil after twenty years of Africa; one source suggests he was married there, returned to England for a while and then emigrated finally to America. Young William is very real to me. It's intriguing that he may have talked with Piet Retief.

I think about William's conversation with the Boers at Dingane's *kraal* on the day before the massacre. He calls these men 'farmers', the literal translation, but 'Boers' has a much wider resonance. To this day many blacks use the word as an insult indicating a rough and unregenerate Afrikaner. There are plenty of those around, and my Cousin Jaco is one of them.

> *On the morning of the third day, I perceived from Dingaan's manner that he meditated some mischief, although from his conversation with his captains I could not perceive that he had given them any orders prejudicial to the farmers. I, however, watched my opportunity to warn them to be on their guard. This occurred when some of the farmers strolled into the* kraal, *and, having come near the place where I was standing, I told them I did not think all was right, and recommended them to be on their guard; upon which they smiled and said: 'We are sure the King's heart is right with us, and there is no cause for fear.'*

William also describes in detail his last meeting with Dingane, who seemed genuinely to like the boy:

> *I must here observe that Dingaan was averse to my going, and told me that during the time I had been with him I had received nothing but kindness; that I had been allowed to do as I liked; that he had given me a herd of cattle, and a number of boys as 'companions'; and he then asked why I wished to go away from him, telling me at the same time that I could do just as I liked, but he would much rather that I should stay. I told him that, having seen the farmers killed, I was so filled with fear that now I could not be happy any longer, and wished much to go to my father at Natal.*

*'Well,' said he, 'I am sorry you are going; but if you are not happy,
I will not detain you.'*

This remarkable boy made his escape. The Zulus were known
to be heading for Port Natal after defeating the revenge party.
William and all the other whites, including the Reverend Francis
Owen's wife and retainers, boarded a ship called the *Comet*,
which was fortuitously tied up in Port Natal. The ship headed
south for safety. The Zulus held the town for nine days before
going back into the interior. The small settlement was destroyed.
Zulu warriors were reported to be wearing the women's crino-
lines they had salvaged.

'What are you reading, *älskling*?' Nellie asks me.

'It is something I asked Liz to scan: she emailed it. It's about
William Wood, the boy who witnessed the massacre. He was
twelve. It's made me think that we should go on a road trip to
where the massacre took place. I want to see the site of the *kraal*
and the grave of Piet Retief.'

'Frank, do you feel some sort of relationship with him?'

'I do up to a point. It's a mixed feeling. And also I feel there is
more to this story.'

'I would like to come with you, but not with Isaac. Maybe
Lucinda will come and I can look after Isaac. You could talk
to Lucinda. It worries me that we don't even know who Isaac is.
We can't take him around the country. How long is Lucinda
staying? I mean when will she take him home?'

'I don't know.'

'Can you ask her?'

151

'I have, Nellie. It's not easy; I love her but she drives me to distraction. The good news is that she says she is now totally laid-back. She's chilling, like totally, to use her exact words. Let's just take it easy and see how the kids are.'

'Bertil is keen to get back to Cape Town, I think.'

'I wonder why? I once read someone describing young Parisians as kissing carnivorously. That's them.'

'Are you a little jealous?'

'I am not jealous. A little envious of how young they are, maybe, but not jealous. I have you.'

'Did I save you from a sad old age?'

'Probably. But I am still a beast in bed.'

'Can you demonstrate that one day? How does that work?'

'Why are you laughing?'

'I'm happy. I am going with the flue.'

'The flow.'

I am terrified that Bertil or Lucinda will hear us making love. They will think it is entirely inappropriate and embarrassing.

'How's the flue?'

'Oh, very good. Very, very good. *Tack så mycket.*'

'*Tack* to you.'

The door opens and Isaac walks into our room, clutching a teddy bear. His face is slightly damp – it has a sheen – and his eyes are fevered.

'Hello, Grandpa, how are you?'

'I'm fine, little Isaac.'

'Can I get in the bed with you?'

'Of course you can, darling,' says Nellie, sliding as unobtrusively as possible off me. We help him into the bed and we feel blessed.

For the first time I notice his hands; it strikes me that they are out of scale. His fingers are long and delicate, as pianists' fingers are said to be. Although I once saw Alfred Brendel play and his fingers seemed to me perfectly normal. I was four rows back, so I can't be sure. Nellie goes to get Isaac a damp cloth for his face and some water to drink, but by the time she comes back Isaac is asleep. He lies on his back, clasping the bear. And I think here, in our fastness, of the comforting role of the teddy bear in English literature. Some of my English friends had made a fetish of their teddy bears at boarding school, allotting them soothing properties and finding them good listeners. The bears were a substitute for lost family life. Sebastian Flyte's Aloysius, Baloo, Paddington and many more – they were all good eggs, standing proxy in their woolly disguise for the best qualities of human beings.

And so we sleep, fitfully, because Isaac kicks every so often as if shocked by an electric charge.

15

Jaco has had an issue for some time with the names of buildings and roads and so on being changed.

Johannesburg Airport used to be called Jan Smuts, now it's called O. R. Tambo. Jan Smuts was a traitor to his people but never mind. What Oliver Tambo knows about aviation is anybody's fucking guess – also he spent most of his life in England. Oom Frank went to Lusaka with other big businessmen to meet Tambo and Mbeki and all them in Zambia years ago. It was a con. *Verneukery*. We was asleep while they was lining themselves up for big jobs and directors of mining companies and so on and guess what, the Jews what owns the big companies is delighted to hand over shares, even whole companies to these top ANC cunts so as to make sure they forget everything they learned in Moscow about communism so they can become fat cats. That is the true story never mind the fucking rainbow nation. So I says Oliver Tambo – *my gat*. My arse.

When a check-in dolly tells me I must not go on board because she says I is drunk I tell her to fuck off – half the people on the plane is pissed anyways, it's all free so what's the fucking difference. She is black but she speaks *deftige* English like some of them does now. Would you mind waiting for a few moments, sir, while I call my supervisor, she calls, and ten seconds later security arrives running and they only tells me I must take a breathalyser test fuck that. Then one of the security *outjies* takes me by the arm. *Kom boet*, he says, he is an Afrikaner like me and he says just sit down for a while, my bru, and I will make it come right for you but you must drink a whole bottle of water then we try the breathalyser again. The Afrikaans guy is quite old he says he lost his job in the pass office in '97 and now he is a security *ouk*. *Ons is nou die kaffers*, he says. We are the kaffers now.

He gives me his card and takes me to another check-in and I get my boarding pass. He tells me not to drink on the plane. I can take this from him but it's sad the kaffers have him by the short and curlies, where's he going to go at fifty-seven? Cape Town International Airport is the only one what does not have the name of some so to say ANC hero on it. I call Oom Frank and he says he is on his way back from scoping the elephants and we can meet tomorrow at Groot Constantia under the trees by the café at 10.30. Great view, he says. A great view is just what I want. Don't worry, he will pay for a taxi. Great, I says, but I am thinking he can ask me to stay the night after I have seen the radio peoples. I would ask you to come to stay, he says, but my daughter is in a very fragile state. Give her a *klap* is my advice but of course I doesn't say that. There's a lot of things I can't say no more.

A pretty girl meet me by the studio, what a pleasure to meet you, she says, my name is Ashlee. She asks if I want a coffee. For why, I wonder. Maybe she thinks I am pissed. Yes please. White please four sugar. Okay, Garry will come down soon to brief you and then it's straight into the studio. Are you all right? *Bakgat*. Scuse me. No fine. She says aren't you the guy who was half eaten by a shark? No, not me. She is a bit confused and turns over her notes then she looks at me: I thought you had lost a leg. No, they is all here all two. I'm the guy who filmed the great white shark and poked it in the eye. My name is Jaco Retief. Two million hits on YouTube. She says two million, omigod that's like amazing. Wow. I will tell Garry. Can you wait here for a bit, Jaco. Chelsee will bring you the coffee and some biscuits if you want. Okay, *lekker*. She has a very short skirt and a tight butt, they always have beautiful girls in these studios. Cherries. She comes back: I forgot, the researcher said you was saying great whites should be shot if they come near a beach, please go a bit easy on that kind of thing. Garry says let's hear the pros and cons of conservation before you say that sort of thing, okay. What is the pros for allowing huge sharks to eat swimmers I ask her. Just saying, she says, just saying take it gently we don't want everybody shouting at once in the studio and don't drink please. Who says I am drinking? Nobody, it's like one of our rules here, no alcohol in the studio.

16

I am waiting under an ancient oak tree, in front of a café, also hundreds of years old, part of the original wine cellars. Resting behind us, magnificent and at its ease, is an old Cape Dutch house. This antiquity is what gives Cape Town its distinction.

I am not looking forward to seeing Jaco. I listened to his programme about sharks on the radio and he sounded as if he had drunk too much, way too much. He made no sense at all and enraged some of the other participants. One of them was a professor from the University of Grahamstown, following in the footsteps of Professor J. L. B. Smith who first recognised the coelacanth for what it was, a fish believed to have died out thousands of years ago, the missing link of fish.

Two ichthyologists and some conservationists argued that the habits of great white sharks should be better understood before slaughter was encouraged. Shark nets were being tried out at the beach where most attacks had taken place.

Jaco intervened. 'Listen,' he said. 'You are talking rubbish, total *kak*. I have nearly been eaten by one of these bastards. I have seen them close up. It's on YouTube. Two million hits. Great whites is killers. That's their job, to kill. It's them or us. You tree-huggers think everything will turn out just fine. These fish is never going to change, either we kill them or we accept that they will go on killing two, three, four, ten people every year. If that's okay with you it's okay with me. Studying their habits is not going to change nothing. They has evolved theirselves for thousands of years. They is made to kill. You can't speak to them or train them like dolphins.'

Two or three in the audience clapped at this; most were angry. The academics ignored Jaco now, no doubt finding him an embarrassment. I felt sorry for Jaco when he tried to enter the conversation about scientific study and tagging. It was clear he wanted all these sharks killed. When the scientist said they were beautiful creatures, he said, 'I can tell you they is not so beautiful when they is coming to rip you into two pieces. I can tell you because I have been there.' It was said in the aggressive, assertive tone of someone who has lost the audience and knows it.

Jaco comes walking up through the avenue of oak trees from the direction of the slave bell. His walk is strangely uneven, as though he has lost the art of putting one foot in front of the other without having to think. I haven't seen him since Tannie Marie's funeral, and in that time he has visibly deteriorated. He looks like a drunk. When he was in England, he was almost preternaturally innocent, a sort of unreformed backwoodsman, excessively muscled and healthy-looking. Brimming with good health.

His ordeal in California and his failure to make anything of his shark experiences seem to have aged him strikingly. His face, even from a distance, is visibly threaded with small veins and his eyes are watery and unclear. He may have been drinking. When we shake hands, last night's alcoholic fumes are still clinging to the wreck of Jaco Retief.

'Hello, Jaco. Sorry to drag you here.'

'No, Oom, it's only a pleasure to see you.'

'I listened to your show the other night.'

'Was it okay? I don't know all the time what they was saying.'

'You aren't the only one. You were good.'

'*Ag*, thanks, man.'

'What's the situation in Potch? Have you got something to do there?'

I am interested in the farm. Jaco lights a cigarette and draws deeply. His fingers are ochre-coloured.

'No. I help on the farm and so on, but the brothers doesn't really want me around. They says Jaco, you fucked off to be a big shot, now when you are on your arse you want something. Anyway, the cousins must sell if they can.'

'Jaco, look, I have been thinking about this possible account of your time in Scientology. I don't believe it's a good idea. If you attack them there may be all kinds of denial and innuendo.'

'What issit? In-new what?'

'Sorry, *innuendo*, it's like suggesting, like hinting, you are this or that; gay, or an alcoholic or something.'

'Number one, I can promise you I am not gay, that's for sure. I hate *mofgats*. And number two, I'm not drinking so much like before. Only white wine with friends.'

'Jaco, I am not saying you are drinking. I don't know anything about you. All I am saying is that the Church of Scientology doesn't like people who blow the whistle on them. Anything can happen. There is no good outcome. I think you should forget it. The journalist who wants to interview you is probably out of a regular job and he will be looking for a sensation so that he can make some money. He will want to use you to tell about what went on, the more bizarre the better. It will all be attributed to you. That's my opinion anyway. You asked me.'

'Thanks for your advice, Oom.'

I order another muffin and some coffee for Jaco. They go in for heavy muffins like bricks around here. Jaco is dejected. I am not sure what he was hoping for; perhaps he thought I would take a look at his contract or have a word in the ear of a big cheese in a London publishing house. Jaco's world has undergone a separation from the real world. And I know that I should cut myself off from him too. But I remember his mother, one of those crushed but sweet women who lived a life of uncomplaining drudgery and boredom on a farm, not too different from Tannie Marie's life. Living on the farm was a kind of imprisonment and farm women were given limited responsibilities, most of which involving appeasing and serving the men. It strikes me now after all these years that it wasn't only the black people who were enslaved although I didn't realise it at the time.

Potchefstroom may be the worst place on earth to come home for Jaco after his traumatic experiences, with the radiance of his brief fame dimmed, his cousins shunning him, his qualifications nil, black people occupying all the traditional jobs. And who knows where his blonde children are.

Jaco looks around aimlessly, unfocused.

Suddenly at our table under the trees we are accompanied by an eager and derisive chorus of the ring-necked turtle doves and the ever-curious guinea fowl. Jaco begins to sob. I take him by the arm and steer him gently to a bench away from the café.

'Oom, I was *kak*. I know. I should of shut my big mouth. I was nervous so I was drinking. I was drunk and they pissed me off. I was the hell in. Thanks for speaking nicely about me but I was shit.

You know when I was with the Scientologists I believed all that crap. I was going to fly to Mars using only my mental powers. Jissus, I have been so fucking stupid always looking for the quick fix and always ending up in the shit. Please help me, Oom. Please. I am begging you.'

Mucus is flowing from his nose to be joined by the tears that are rolling unstoppably from his injured eyes to form a small delta above his mouth. The injury to his eyes is a psychological one, a kind of accumulating wariness. They are the eyes of self-loathing and failure.

A small group of middle-aged, upper-class English tourists pass us, speaking loudly and confidently.

One, in a light anorak, says, *The British planted these oaks for the Royal Navy's use, you know. But they grew too fast out here in the sun and they were no use for building ships.*

Jolly interesting, Simon, but we need a drink pronto.

Right, the wine-tasting cellar is just here. We have a choice, the wine-tasting after the big house or the wine-tasting before the big house? Yes, all right, I know it is a damn silly question. This way.

On behalf of Jaco, I find myself bristling at their loud and ineffably confident pronouncements. They are mostly wearing walking boots as if they were going to do some climbing. In a very English way they glance surreptitiously at the stricken Jaco as they pass. Jaco is trying unsuccessfully to regain his composure as he gulps for air. I am desperately sorry for him, but I also feel urgently the need to protect my family from exposure to him. He is out of control. He's dangerous.

I speak to him in Afrikaans as if that will be more welcome, more soothing.

'*Kom, Jaco, kom ons daar onder die eikebome sit. Kom nou.*' Come, Jaco, let's sit over there under the oak trees. Come now.

I don't want him to be seen crying in full view. He stumbles after me and we sit on a bench under the oaks. He apologises again. After a while he stops sobbing. I see the plight of Jaco as symbolic of a wider tragedy, one that is way beyond Jaco's comprehension. I think, in the midst of the choking sobs, of Piet Retief, and I wonder if our ancestor was really just an innocent, shaped by Bible stories and obsessed by the belief that God was reserving a *Heimat* expressly for his people.

In his manifesto justifying his emigration from the Cape Colony, he wrote:

> *We complain of the severe losses which we have been forced to sustain by the emancipation of our slaves and the vexatious laws which have been enacted respecting them. We complain of the continuous system of plunder which we have ever endured from the Caffres and other coloured classes, and particularly by the last invasion of the colony.*

On this evidence, it seems unlikely that Retief was proposing to live in a free state with the Zulus. There is nothing in his history, including his advocacy on behalf of slave owning, that suggests he would have lived peaceably with the Zulus. Dingane understood this.

And here is poor Jaco, the product of this immense and fatal misunderstanding, a victim of the consequent culture clash, of hundreds of years of unthinking brutality and plunder, of slavery and exploitation and betrayal. Dingane's disquiet was at least understandable. He already possessed the perfect universe, with his beautiful cattle and the elaborate ritual that surrounded them, his scores of wives, his thousands of warriors, his medicine men and his vast savannahs, deep forests and magical rivers. He did not want anything to change. He had no good reason to welcome the white man in the person of my ancestor: *I see that every white man is an enemy to the black, and every black man an enemy to the white. They do not love each other and never will.*

Who could blame Dingane for murdering Retief? Not me. Yet my ancestor has a huge statue in his honour at the Voortrekker Memorial, as if he were a hero. It stands, forming a corner of the monument. It's a monument to delusion. But then many monuments are.

A pigeon lands at our feet; it waddles complacently a little closer, perhaps in search of crumbs or peanuts, which are known as 'monkey nuts' in these parts. Suddenly Jaco swipes violently at the pigeon, which flies away in alarm. He punches the bench. Hitting hard objects in frustration is an American habit; perhaps he learned it in California. I am startled by this pent-up emotion. I think that in his imagining he was striking me or Dingane or some of those black people who are wandering so confidently around their own country. He has hurt his hand, and holds it tenderly. This, too, happens in American movies.

'I'm going to Potchefstroom now-now,' he says.

'Jaco, I will think about what I can do for you, but in the meanwhile I have to look after my daughter. She's not stable. Here's some money for a taxi to the airport and some more.'

I give him a bundle of notes.

'No, I can't take that.'

'Take it, Jaco.'

His hands are trembling as he reaches for the money.

'*Baie dankie, Oom.*'

'I'm not your uncle. Try to remember that. You'll get a taxi over there where the tourists are dropped off.'

He gets to his feet with difficulty. He looks at me for a moment. He forms his mouth into a shape that suggests that he has a final thank-you – or curse – for me. But then he walks off unsteadily, and I will never know what he was proposing to say.

There are no guarantees that he will not drink the money.

As I drive back over the pass in the direction of home, I recall Retief's last point in his manifesto:

We are now quitting the fruitful land of our birth, and are entering a wilderness and dangerous territory; but we go with a firm reliance on an all-seeing, just, and merciful Being, whom it will be our endeavour to fear and humbly to obey.

I swoop down the mountain, through the forest, past the old winery, past Mandela Park, past the road to the harbour, and I rise up beneath Little Lion's Head which does look from certain directions uncannily like a huge lion reclining while staring into the distance. Exactly like the lions in Trafalgar Square.

On the way down to the sea I give Nellie an account of my meeting with Jaco and I assure her that he is safely on his way home via Johannesburg Airport. Oliver Tambo Airport.

Our trip to the Addo Elephant Park was a huge success although Bertil was a little restless, perhaps keen to get back to Vanessa.

Nellie and the others have all fallen in love with elephants. Elephants radiate a sense of contentment and good will. Like whales, they offer a kind of example for us. Nellie tells me that she finds the way they take care of the young elephants and the way they reassure each other with a caress from a trunk or with a rumbling call, especially moving. The guide said they have many different calls, rumbles and screeches. He called these noises 'harmonics', most of them not audible to human beings. Bertil has been patient and helpful with Isaac, also somewhat caught up in the mystery of Isaac's provenance. Isaac hero-worships him.

The Elephant Park is vast – nearly half a million acres. The mountains are covered by tough green trees, dropping vertiginously into ravines, and the coastline is wild and rugged, a landscape of forests and enormous sand dunes in some parts; in others there are water holes and flat prairie. We stayed the night in a renovated farmhouse; with its tin roof and wide veranda it reminded me keenly of the farm and Tannie Marie reading *Pinocchio* to me by candlelight. She loved me and it was cruel of my father to remove me for ever from her after my mother died, but perhaps there is more to that story than I know or will ever know.

We saw lions and rhino and buffaloes as well as the elephants in the Addo Elephant Park. I wondered if the lions were causing havoc amongst the antelope. Perhaps they were fed out of sight. The park boasts of conserving the whales, penguins, gannets and great white sharks off its shores. There are plans to proclaim a vast marine sanctuary. We were shown the unique Addo flightless dung beetle. It has a comical, stiff-legged gait, as if it were running on tiny stilts. Sadly it was not at that time rolling up dung, which is the dung beetle's party trick. It's all admirable in a way, but I am not sure Nellie understands the subtext, which is to keep as much of this part of Africa pristine and free of the poor in general and squatters in particular. Vast tracts of land are being set aside in the name of conservation.

I had believed that the new nation was going to be a miracle. My eyes were opened early, in 1990, when I was invited by the ANC to the ceremony marking the return of the body from Conakry, West Africa, of Tsietsi Mashinini, the schoolboy hero of the Soweto Uprising. I was asked because I had raised funds for the ANC in London; for years I was on committees. Although Tsietsi was a member of Black Consciousness, the ANC hijacked the event. When the coffin was opened it was discovered that there was an unexplained hole in the back of Tsietsi's head and one of his eyes had been pushed right in. His face had suffered a deep wound and his forehead was scarred. What happened to him in those thirteen years is a mystery.

I began to question the tale of heroic resistance. To tell the truth, I never really went along with the myth of the struggle; it seemed to me to be largely symbolic. I was in Johannesburg when a bomb went off near the Town Hall in 1994. The young white boys in uniform were terrified. Nobody knew what was coming next. There were rumours that the far right had planted the bomb. As I drove away fast in my hire car, I saw fires in petrol drums and groups of men huddled around them, wrapped in blankets against the cold. It was a sight that I felt I had seen many times in television news reports, turmoil and terror shrouded in the fog of dust and mortar that explosives create. When I stopped for a red light, a man swathed in a grey blanket ran towards me holding a cane-cutting machete. I raced away, unnerved; in that moment I understood how fear could unhinge you: shaking uncontrollably, I sped back to the white and comfortable and prosperous suburbs.

I don't tell Nellie these dark stories. She prefers the story of a rainbow nation, and who can blame her? She is on holiday, not on a fact-finding mission.

17

Jaco is speaking to his wife. He says he misses the children. They are nearly four and three years, he thinks. Or maybe five and four. He's not a hundred per cent sure. A lot has happened.

Elfrieda, he says, I miss the children.

Kak. You buggered off with a whore with big boobs from Sun City. Now she knows that you are a *dronk-lap* and a liar she don't want to speak to you.

That's all *kak*.

I didn't make it up, I heard the truth. I know what happened, Jaco. Also when I was working in Nelspruit at the hairdresser and looking after the children where were you when they was crying in their bed? I can tell you, you was in California being a big shot. *Ooo, vok die* great white is going to bite my balls off. God *verskoon my*, I wish the shark had eaten your *balletjies*. True's God. And you were drunk when you was talking crap about sharks on the radio the other day, everyone was ashamed of you. *Dank die Here* that your children is too young to know what a *poes* you is.

Elfrieda, listen, I made mistakes no question everybody makes mistakes but now I want to see my daughters and you if you can forgive me.

Fuck off, Jaco. Why don't you fly off to Mars like what you said you can do – you are a loser and a liar.

Whosez?

Your cousins on the farm and everyone what we knows. All you want is to get the money what I have saved for the children. Stay away.

Elfrieda, I have money.

I am getting married, says Elfrieda.

What did you say?

I'm getting married to Wynand Vermeulen.

Jaco puts the phone down.

Married, never. It can't be true.

Jannie holds his hand out. It's not Jaco's phone. He borrowed it from Jannie. He left his on the plane or somewhere. He has talked to Elfrieda for twenty minutes and Jannie wants him to pay now–now. He's sitting in the Bourbon Street trying to get the amount what he owes from MTN so he can pay Jannie.

Jannie takes the phone. He is a tight-arse.

Jaco feels sick. Married. How come?

Jannie says it's twenty-five rand. Jaco gets out the roll of notes his uncle gave him. It is not as fat as he remembers. He peels off a twenty. And here's ten for old times. Why you surprised, Jannie? You was thinking I am going to run, *neh*? You do me a favour I do you a favour, ou pal.

Jaco and Stoffel stand up to leave the pub.

Still whatever she says I want to see my children. Six months that he has not seen them. Also I will like to kill Elfrieda who is a *hoer*. She fucked everyone who was around in Nelspruit as I am told but still she gets the hell in really mad when she hear about this girl Casey at Sun City. Never mind that, it was nothing, *niks nie, een*-night stand, maybe a few more who's counting. Nothing.

Women doesn't unnerstan most men need more than one woman no harm done. Except that she told one of her friends who was in PR at Sun City. She only went and tell the newspaper *Shark-man plays away from home*. Can you believe that. I want to kill the journalis who wrote that. You cunt, I have children. How can you do that to my children?

Bang bang.

I wish.

Jaco feels better with his gun in his trousers strapped to his thigh. It makes his thigh warm. It's one up at all times. He likes to know it is there. We must look after ourself now. There's a lot of reasons to carry a gun with all that's going on here, the Congo people who are cannibals where they comes from and all the Zim people who are not so bad but they can't get jobs up there so they swim across the Limpopo, nobody knows how many has been eaten by crocs. That *poes* Zuma gives all the jobs to his buddies from Zululand. One day they is sitting on their arse in Zululand the next they flying first class to Paris for a conference talk talk talk talk. That is what they likes most, talk talk talk. All what Zuma does now is to jump around wearing feathers and leopard skins and then they all drinks beer and kills an ox and cooks it. The President is the chief so he gets the liver. He has twenty-one or twenty-two kids. Maybe more. When a white guy applies for a job his application goes to the bottom of the pile. Sorry it's lost. Jissus I would like to kill them all. That *mofgat* de Klerk gave the whole country away for nothing. Did Oliver Tambo build Union Buildings? No he fucking did not. I am a Retief and we doesn't forget what they did to Piet; he had to watch Zuma's ancestors kill a hundred and fifty men, women and children. Little childrens like my girls

clubbed with a knobkerrie. My beautiful daughters Elmarie and ...
what's her name oh *ja*, June. Junie like Junie Carter.

Jannie and Stoffel is going home.

Cheer up, says Stoffel, it could be worse.

How?

I don't know.

Let's go and shoot some great whites.

Very funny. Fuck off.

18

Bertil is surfing with Vanessa. He really can surf after two weeks. Surfing has taken him over. He spends hours in the surf. Now he is wearing a T-shirt which reads *It is not tragic to die doing something you love*. Nellie is a little nervous. I promise to speak to Vanessa to make sure that a life-saver is always around when Bertil is surfing. He hasn't yet tried to ride the very big breakers that come roaring towards the beach. He makes a good job of the smaller waves. I can see that his eyes are on the big surf, which can be terrifying. Bertil tells me, without irony, that surfing is a 'post-capitalism pastime'. I think he means that it is another way of seeing the world; that the objectives of surfing are entirely personal, without rules; that the ocean is absolutely free and democratic; that it gives no special favours to bankers ... et cetera.

Little Isaac wants to surf too. He stands on the beach watching Vanessa and Bertil. They wave to him from the deep water. I take him on a body-board in shallow water with a rope attached and launch him into the gentle waves. He tries to stand up, but so far standing up is beyond him. I show him how I body-surf, without a board at all, but he is not interested. He wants to be a surf dude riding the big waves. It is heart-rending how persistent he is and how often and how cheerfully he falls off the board. God, he is two and a half years old. I too have found myself becoming besotted with him. Bertil and Vanessa often come onto the beach to talk to him and to help him. He is like the baby Jesus, suggesting some special insight. He seems wonderfully happy among us. He calls Lucinda 'Mom'; there is no mention of another mother. Nellie and I have stopped worrying about where he should be by rights. We have become unnaturally, even culpably, relaxed. Lindiwe is trying to teach Isaac some Xhosa, as if he should be able to speak it because he is black. Actually 'black' doesn't quite describe Isaac. His skin is honey-coloured. His hair has become reddish. Lucinda swims every day now. We are all in thrall to the sea and its magical powers.

I have the idea that I should travel to Natal to see Piet Retief's grave. I am not sure what I am hoping to find. I see that Nellie and Lucinda don't really want to come; I detect a little weariness when I bring up Piet's name. So I suggest we all fly to Durban and book into a hotel so that Bertil can surf, Isaac can paddle, and Lucinda and Nellie can relax on the beach or in the hotel's swimming pool. And I will set off early in the morning to see the grave, alone if nobody else wants to come, and I will return in the evening. I agree that I should take a driver.

I remember from my childhood only one of Durban's aspects, the rickshaws on the seafront, pulled by Zulus dressed in extravagant versions of traditional dress, all feathers and porcupine quills and beadwork. The rickshaw men in those days had cow horns on their heads. These rickshaws were once the taxis of Durban, but for many years now they have been a local entertainment, taking tourists for an energetic ride along the front. We watch as they parade, leaping in the air, whistling and shouting as if they were going into battle.

Nellie thinks it would be demeaning to the men to take a ride. On the other hand, we would be supporting local initiative. Isaac and I take a ride and he loves it. He waves at Nellie and Lucinda as we go floating by, and he laughs when our driver leaps in the air blowing a whistle and we can see the ocean through his legs. The air here is heavy and steamy indicating that we have wandered into the tropics. We all go down to the beach to cool off; Bertil wants to try the surfing; he has researched it online and he knows exactly where the best surfing is, Veetchies Break. Surfers have their occult networks. Isaac has an ice cream, which quickly melts onto his vulnerable little chicken chest. Suddenly I see to my amazement Bertil catching a long break and riding it at speed. He is our hero. In a few weeks he has become muscled and brown and quietly pleased with himself. He has the surfer look, a tolerant, visionary appearance. His hair is bleached by the sun and by the ocean.

'Did you know you could do that?' I ask him when he comes out of the surf, shaking the water from his head.

'I was like hoping to try one of these breaks I had read about and we just took off.'

'You looked so good, Bertil,' said Nellie. 'For a moment I couldn't believe it when Frank said it was you.'

'I recognised you by your cozzie. The flying palm trees.'

'It was luck really,' says Bertil. But we are not fooled.

Lucinda is by the pool at the hotel. We tell her about Bertil's triumph. She congratulates him as if it is a major development. He smiles modestly.

'You are one cool dude,' she says. 'Nellie, will you be able to look after Isaac if I go with Dad tomorrow to wherever it is he is going?'

'Of course, darling. I would love to look after him.'

I have been waiting for an opportunity to speak to Lucinda and I am glad that she suggested coming with me. What my father would have called a proper conversation. So far she has still been something of a wraith, not wholly with us. But she has been amiable and content, which is enough for me at this time. I see that this place has had a profound effect on all of us. Living by the sea seems to encourage us to follow its rhythms and to have an awareness of the tides and waves that mark the hours.

Landscapes, I think, remind one of home and encourage a longing to be home. When I am at my house under the mountain, by the sea, I feel that I am home, despite the violence and the desperation that are never far away.

19

Lucinda and I leave early in the morning, trusting ourselves to Gibson, the driver, who wears a smart uniform, a blue safari-suit, and a nautical cap. Off we go into the hopeful morning, heading north along the coast. Already some surfers are out. The sea has a blue-green colour this morning. It is more tropical than where we come from. The waves are small, the sea calm. Little knots of men, standing at the water's edge, are casting with huge rods, deep into the waves. A fisherman pulls in a large silver fish, struggling hopelessly. In that instant we fly by and the fish story is incomplete, for ever a fleeting image.

We are soon travelling through sugar-cane plantations. Way inland we can see a thunderstorm; the distant rain has given the sky a cross-hatched appearance. Gibson says it is moving, towards the Drakensberg. I wonder how the trekkers coped on those mountains in their wagons when these fierce thunderstorms struck.

'Those are the mountains that Piet Retief came down when he was looking for somewhere to settle. Over in that direction.'

'Why are you doing this, Dad? Really?'

Lucinda's face is sleepy and clouded and warm, and she sits with her legs folded under her and her head on my shoulder. I wonder if she has recovered completely; I hope that this is not just a period of remission. It has been a terrible hell to see my beloved daughter slipping into irrationality; who would blame me if I chose to believe that she will soon be herself again?

'Why do you ask?'

'You are a sly old fox, aren't you? You have always had your own private thoughts and ideas. What's this Zulu outing really all about, Daddy?'

'I don't have a secret agenda. Or any fixed agenda. It's just that, as time goes by, I feel the urge to make my peace. I have been thinking about it almost every day. Going to see my – our – ancestor's grave may help. I believe in serendipity, so I am sure it will be worthwhile. But the truth, darling, is that I am basically just curious. I always want to get a sense of what a place is like.'

'Are you ashamed of being Piet Retief's descendant or are you kinda pleased, like people who are related to Billy the Kid or Bonnie and Clyde?'

'Look, Retief was a bankrupt who left the Cape Colony, recklessly taking his children and followers with him; his son, Cornelis, was one of the seventy killed, followed by another hundred or so servants, women and children, all because Retief was naïve, convinced he had a real treaty with Dingane, and also because he thought that God was on his side. Unfortunately, neither was true. I am pretty sure his plan was to take Dingane's country. Does that sound to you like someone I should admire?'

'Probably not.'

Perversely, I do value my relation with Retief, as if it gives me some substance, some authenticity, some purchase on this land. For better or for worse I am descended from pioneers. In its own way it is like having ancestors who landed at Cape Cod in the *Mayflower*. (Although they had intended to land in Virginia.) 'And, by the way, there is some evidence that the treaty a party of Boers claimed to have found months later was a fake.'

The landscape unrolls, gloriously.

'Do you love Nellie?'

'What a strange question.'

'Not so strange. I think she is great. Like the best thing that could have happened.'

She holds my hand just as she did when she was a child, with a light but persistent grip. And now I can see her as a four-year-old, eager, always cheerful, building houses with cushions and chairs and blankets to hide in, and singing loudly and raucously from inside her hide-away.

And soon after her fourth birthday, Georgina and I started our war.

'I do love Nellie, darling. Yes. She has made me calm after all those years with your mother. I have never blamed your mother, by the way, it was just that we were a total mismatch. I am as much to blame. Maybe more so.'

'Dad, I have wanted to ask you this for a long time ...' I brace myself. 'Did my drug phase have anything to do with the break-up?'

I take comfort from the words 'drug phase' because it suggests she thinks it is all over.

'No, darling. It was never your fault. You watched, appalled. I thought you went off the rails because of our rows. Was it awful for you at home?'

'It was pretty bad but I was always on your side, Daddy. You know that. Mum seemed to like enjoy arguments. Whatever we said, she contradicted us or she had a better idea. Whatever I wanted to do, even finger painting when I was three, she would like take over and tell me how to do it properly. And she always wanted me to dress like her, boots and furs and big necklaces even when I was five or six. Beautiful mother with beautiful daughter. I was just an accessory.'

'I am so sorry.'

I know it's true.

She is looking out of the window now towards the storm. It has moved away so that all we see of it is a smudge on the horizon. As we turn off the coastal road and head inland, Gibson says we have another hour and a half to go. I ask him about his family and his home. He glances at me in the mirror.

'I am from Ladysmith, sir. I have four children.' (He pronounces it 'chill-ren'.) 'Two boys and two daughters, sir.'

We stop for a break above a river, shaded by a single tree. Gibson says there are still a few crocodiles down there. On the other side of the river is a *kraal* of round, traditional, thatched huts and a few mud huts with corrugated-iron roofs, held in place by rocks. Startlingly bright kingfishers dive into the water from their perch on a dead tree. They are like bright Christmas decorations. *Chill-ren* emerge from the *kraal* and hop across towards us on huge, worn, red boulders. A small grey dog swims across, paddling fiercely and optimistically. I hope there are no crocodiles just here. Gibson has sandwiches and water for us in a coolbox and some sweets and drinks for the children. But when they ask for money he is severe, and they retreat, chastened. They watch us from within an anxious little circle. Lucinda is all for digging into her tote bag for money, but Gibson says it is not good for them to beg.

Lucinda gives the remains of a sandwich to the dog, which has correctly identified her as a soft touch. The dog suddenly shakes itself violently, wetting Lucinda. She laughs. Gibson is concerned and produces a roll of kitchen towel. He warns that some of these dogs have rabies.

On we go, blissful. Lucinda is sleeping; it is the sleep of the innocent; I am almost convinced that she is recovering. Of course I can't judge whether the effects of drugs will linger, nor if her brain has been altered for ever in some way. The brain is a mystery to me, both in its workings and in its symbolism. Scientists say it has a mind of its own.

While my troubled daughter sleeps, I watch the landscape unfurling; for my own amusement I try to name birds and spot weaver-bird nests hanging over water and I look out for meerkats and old farmhouses and early roads and abandoned cement bridges that are now bypassed, and trading stores and Nguni cattle and signs of Voortrekker roads and mission churches and women walking stoically as we throw up dust around them and the darting leaping flight of impala and snakes on the road and ant hills and donkeys ridden by children or pulling carts and school children in uniform and the signposts to farms and millenarian missions. There are plenty of missions of this sort. It seems that the poorer you are the more you are likely to turn to bogus religions for some sort of comfort. It may be that my ancestor and those who came after him destroyed a thousand years of belief and custom, which interpreted and contained all that was required for the life the Zulus lived. Denigrating the indigenous peoples and their customs was one of the worst crimes of colonialism.

'Are we nearly there?'

'Oh, hello, sweetheart. Yes, nearly there.'

'Lovely sleep. I read somewhere that sleep is a brief respite from mortality.'

'I like that.'

She places her head on my lap and I stroke her hair. I am seized by optimism; I feel it is me as much as Lucinda who is coming alive after a long hibernation.

We drive down a very bumpy track, past a mission, and stop under some trees. Gibson leads us on foot in the direction of Dingane's *kraal*. We pass through a palisade of large dried branches. Gibson says that the *kraal* is being re-created as accurately as possible. The *kraal*, the *isigodlo*, the heart of Dingane's kingdom, was huge. About ten beehive huts have been built so far. It is wonderfully evocative. Once there were hundreds of beehive huts, for a thousand of the King's trusted warriors and his five hundred women. At the centre of the *isigodlo* was the enclosure for his revered cattle. The King's house is twice as big as any other, and is built exactly on the original site, as indicated by the remains of the wooden posts that held up the beautiful beehive structure. There are no people around at all, but I can easily and vividly imagine the place as a bustling Zulu metropolis.

We look down the hill to the mouth of the *isigodlo*. Eight hundred yards away is the hill called KwaMatiwane, the killing fields. Here thousands were killed over the years. Death was only separated from life by the breath of the King. He could kill on a whim, and did.

'That's where our ancestor died. Young William Wood wrote that Piet was the last one to be clubbed to death, so that he was forced to watch his followers and his son being killed.'

'I don't want to go down there,' says Lucinda.

Gibson drives us to the memorial for Piet Retief and his comrades. It is placed on the crown of a small hill. It is strangely similar to hundreds, even thousands, of memorials in British towns; it is essentially a Victorian memorial in the shape of an obelisk, bearing the names of the seventy Boers who were murdered by Dingane's warriors. A few sentences place the blame on the Zulu king. The citations are written in Dutch. The word '*moord*' – murder – is used.

I hold Lucinda's hand as we gaze at the grave, not communing with our ancestor, but simply overwhelmed by the quietness and emptiness of the landscape and the palpable sense of tragedy, a double tragedy, that took place here. This awful massacre has drained the life out of the surroundings. I am reminded of Terezín, which has a deathly quiet, unable to sustain the weight of its own ignominy. Although the Boers all died, this was also the beginning of the end for the Zulus. I think that this is the birthplace of the notion of the '*swartgevaar*', the black menace, which justified so much cruelty and repression.

On the way to Blood River, I ask Lucinda if she wants to hear my theory.

'Sure. Why not? Your theory about what?'

She looks surprisingly interested in what I have to say.

'About apartheid. I think it was the product of fear. The whites were terrified of the blacks, particularly black men, and the massacre right here was the confirmation the Boers needed that you couldn't trust black people. Never mind what the whites did to the blacks over time, they retained this fear. Retief complained about unruly "*Caffres*" in his manifesto. When he arrived here, hoping to steal Dingane's land and enslave his people, his worst fears of unruly *Caffres* were realised.'

'I don't want to spoil your fun, Dad, but the whole Negro slave era was just the same. There are tons of theses and books about it.'

'Yes, I know, but I am saying that this was the moment, the *moment critique*, that sparked it all off here, a long war, like Gavrilo Princip's assassination of Archduke Franz Ferdinand. Right here on February the 6th, 1838, at an exact moment of time and history, something happened that had terrible and lasting consequences.'

'And our ancestor was to blame.'

'I think he was the catalyst; he blundered in, miscalculated completely, and this fear and loathing led to apartheid and the idea that you needed to control black men at all times or else they would chase you into the sea after raping all your women.'

Subdued, we drive on towards Blood River. I may be imagining a growing closeness between me and Lucinda. I am longing for it.

I give her the background: Blood River was the place where Dingane tried to finish off the Boers for ever. It went very badly for him. The Boers, under Andries Pretorius, had drawn up their sixty-four wagons in a circle, protected on two sides by the Blood River. The Zulus attacked in waves but the Boers fired repeatedly until the Zulus were lying in piles in the river and around the wagons. Three thousand Zulus died while only three Boers were lightly injured, one of them Pretorius. To them this miracle was God's doing and they entered a covenant with him. As a schoolboy I was supposed to acknowledge the Day of the Covenant. It was a holiday; we acknowledged it by taking the day off to surf at Muizenberg, where Bertil had his surfing lessons. In those days nobody had heard of great whites.

The first sight of the sixty-four bronze wagons, full-sized, startles Lucinda. For a few moments she thinks they are real wagons. The wagons are placed in a circle on the bank of the river to commemorate this great day. Each wagon is identical to the others. A small boy of about eight is fashioning clay heads of cattle beyond a fence. As I approach him, he holds up the clay models. I buy them both and give him ten times what he is asking. His little, desperate face collapses. He starts to run in the direction of a village. I don't tell Lucinda that it is in remembrance of the children on Tannie Marie's farm.

An elderly Afrikaner is in charge of the museum. He is wearing the sort of clothing I recognise from my childhood, not so much out of fashion as dredged from deep time. Diffidently he offers to run a short film of the battle, made forty years ago. Yes, please.

When they are shot it's striking how enthusiastically the extras behave in this old film. The Zulu extras pile into the river and fall back into the water dramatically. They attack, futilely, but wholeheartedly. Before they are shot, they hurl their assegais with intent as if they are enjoying a rerun of the original battle. I wonder if they were carried away by the opportunity of a return fixture. The script demands that they fall and play dead, which they do with gusto. The pretend-injured hobble away clutching their wounds on shattered legs. The film is in black-and-white so the eponymous blood is not available, but we can imagine it. For all its old-fashioned technique, the film, like the old man's clothes, touches me.

'Great value, Daddy, two massacres in one day.'

'Don't be so cynical, Lucinda.'

'You have to laugh in the face of disaster. Dad, I have had a great time being with you, and this has been incredible, like absolutely amazing. Just you and me.'

'I'm glad, darling. It's always been you and me.'

She turns away from the landscape to me.

'I know you have been very worried about me.'

'Yes, I have been very worried about you. But that's my job.'

'I am over it, Daddy. I promise. I can see that there is much more to a life. When you are taking drugs you just like lose all proportion. You are looking for smack all day long and it's like nothing else matters. People think heroin is difficult to get off, but it is not so difficult to get off at all, the only thing is that it is much more enticing than real life. When you are clean you feel absolutely useless. It's totally crazy.'

She hugs me and I hold her vulnerable body close. I am careful, as if her body could snap like a twig. As a parent you must console your children at all times.

Gibson, who is a naturally solicitous man, says it would be best to be off these dirt roads before it is dark. Lucinda and I get into the car and huddle together on the back seat, complicit in our special knowledge, all the way to the coast. Gibson passes us the picnic hamper. We tuck in to the sandwiches.

I was elated when Lucinda said she was definitely over her drug phase; all the taut air left me in a rush, like a maverick balloon at a children's party. Now I look at her lovely face, which always recalls the young Georgina. The flickering light catches the bolts in her nose. I say nothing, although I hope she will have them removed.

'I will get rid of them,' she says, seeing me looking too obviously, my gaze, like a moth's, drawn to the light.

We are tired out by important thoughts, unexpected emotions and huge skies. We sleep the sleep of the just, although nothing more than a father and a daughter together again.

20

Jaco is tooled up. He has his 9mm Beretta 92FS semi-automatic strapped to his thigh, ten rounds in the magazine. He is totally pissed off. That fucking bitch won't speak to him. She says he doesn't even know his children's names. What a lot of *kak*. There is only two, Elmarie and June who is named June like Johnny Cash's wife Junie, how can I forget that. What a voice. Junie has a voice like an angel. It juss cut through your feelings so you can change from sad to happy in a blink or go the other way happy to sad. June Carter – Junie. That voice can make you cry. When I was in California I play the soundtrack from the film all the time until they take it away and wants me to go in the E-meter to clean my head. If I would have the Beretta then I would blow their fucking heads off.

It's shit hitch-hiking but the brothers on the farm will not lend me even a *bakkie* nor nothing. *Niks nie.* They want me to piss off and get lost for ever. They say I am giving a bad example to the blacks by fucking Hester and drinking too much. Who cares I am fucking Hester. Anyway I thought this was the new free South Africa, fuck anybody you like, no worries.

He's standing by the road taking a *soepie* from a jack of brandy. Commando Brandy. He's going to rescue his children and take them on holiday. He's still got some of Uncle Frank's cash. Maybe they can go to Durban for a holiday. The people there is called the Banana Boys because they grows bananas there. A black guy stops to pick him up. His car is low on the springs like all these people's cars is. They haven't got a fucking clue how to look after a car. He gets in anyway. The black guy is going some of the way before he turns off. He wants money for sure.

I will give you fifty rand, bru.

OK, sharp.

He's ready, one up just in case. The Beretta is warming his leg.

After a few kilometres the black guy's car has a puncture. Jaco helps him change the tyre. The black guy drops Jaco off at an Engen station. Fuck knows where they are. He asks a driver who is filling up to give him a ride in the cab of his coal truck, because I can see he is Afrikaans. He tells the driver he must see his wife who is having baby number three.

You can't by law sit in the cab.

Listen, my *ou maat*, I must go to Nelspruit. A baby is being born.

And you are one of the fucking Wise Men. Okay I will take you but my arse is grass if they finds out.

Jaco passes him the brandy: have a dop.

Are you fucking crazy? I got three hundred tons of coal in this baby.

What baby?

This truck.

Okay, *ek verstaan*. My *naam* is Retief. Jaco. And yours?

Willem Van Zyl.

They shake hands. The truck roars. Jaco has a *soep* of Commando. It's nearly dark when he arrives in Nelspruit. It's pissing down. The driver wants him to get out without being seen and he stops the truck behind a huge tin-and-brick building with no windows. An abattoir. *Slaghuis.*

I know how dead cattle and sheep is smelling.

Jaco has no idea where Elfrieda lives – he's never been to Nelspruit. He walks to the Wimpy and has a cheeseburger with hot sauce. Just what I need. He washes himself in the lavatory and rinses his mouth. I look like shit. I look old. *Ja*, but a few days in Durban jolling with the Banana Boys will fix me up. Maybe I will take up snorkelling again. He calls Elfrieda's mother, Francine. She thinks she is a Huguenot. She hates him. Jaco says he is sending a present for the girls and he needs the postal address.

Just a minute.

He can hear scratching like mice in the cupboard. The old people is so fucking slow. Scratching and coughing and looking for their fucking glasses. Talking about drink, Francine is a champion.

Orright, Jaco, it is 41 Jacaranda Avenue, Nelspruit 2207.

Baie dankie, hoor, Ma.

I am not your mother.

I know, Ma. When is Elfrieda getting married?

Next week.

What's his name again?

His name is Wynand.

Lovely. Okay, *tot siens, Ouma.*

The line is dead. It's not a problem to find the house. The manager of the Wimpy, an Indian *outjie*, lives in the next street. He gives me a free coffee and a jam doughnut because I am going to be a father. He thinks. He says it is more or less ten minutes to walk. He draws me a map on a paper napkin. He writes also 'congratulations'. That's nice. The streets is quiet. I come there

188

and I see that the lights is on and I climb over the wall and walk through the garden. They doesn't have any security. Maybe it go on later. I stand myself behind a bush covered with red flowers. It's hot here in Nelspruit. I can see in the front room the back of a man. The fucking bridegroom. Wynand. Then I see Elfrieda come in carrying some food on a tray. It looks like it can be a T-bone. The man is staring at the television. His face is flickering. He doesn't look at Elfrieda when he takes his tray he just hold out his hand. He's got *vok*-all manners. I walk to the front door and knock and ring the bell.

Who's there?

Polisie, Specials.

The door comes open a little way on a chain and I push it in no trouble with my shoulder.

Ooh my God, *dis* Jaco. What do you want?

What you think? I have come to see my children.

This Wynand stands up in a hurry. He is a big bastard.

Fuck off out of here, he says.

Who sez?

I says.

He moves towards me. His fly is open. I take the Beretta out of my pants and aim straight at him. Still he comes and I shoot him in the groin area. In the sausage department. Blood, Jissus, it's like a fucking fountain. Elfrieda is screaming.

Shuttup. *Hou op, jou hoer*, the children will wake up.

Are you crazy, you shot Wynand. You shot him.

Get the girls out of bed, I want to see them.

Now because of that *poes* Wynand I can't take the children with. Durban is out. The cops will be looking for me. I must see the children. The children is crying in their room. I want them to shut up and be happy. The boerbull comes out from the kitchen. It makes a horrible noise, its eyes is watery. It stinks of dog shit. I am going to shoot the fucking dog if it try to bite me.

And I want the car keys, Elfrieda.

I say if she calls the police I will kill her. She believes me even if it's not true.

Elfrieda, the children mustn't see Wynand, definitie.

They are at the door staring at me, their eyes like bush babies'.

Hello, girlies, howzit with you? You are coming to stay with me on the farm next Easter, don't be frightened. That's right, *neh*, Elfrieda? Tell the girls.

Yes. We are all going to Daddy's farm.

Is Oom Wynand coming?

No, Elmarie.

Wynand is groaning in the sitting room.

Stay here, don't move.

I go to the sitting room. He's fucked, he's twitching. Probably *gevrek*.

Elfrieda, where's the car – I told you I am taking it. So where is it?

In the carport.

Okay, let's go. Bye bye, girls, see you at Easter. Tell them to say goodbye, Elfrieda.

Say goodbye to your pa.

Bye-bye, bye-bye.

I kiss the girls. They looks *poep* scared. Elfrieda tells them, don't leave your bedroom or I will give you a *klap*.

She's crying and shaking. She takes me to the car, a small Ford. It's a clapped-out piece of shit.

Is it diesel or petrol?

Petrol, Jaco.

Call the ambulance and the police when I has gone. Tell them you was asleep and kaffers stole the car. Don't say I shot Wynand. I wasn't even here, *neh*? You say that a black man came here, you didn't see him but you heard him shouting and Wynand shouting and you have stayed with the girls and then you have heard a noise and then he must've been shot by Wynand. You was too frightened to come out.

Fuck this Wynand. If his fat slang was not peeping out of his pants he will be alive now. And we can be on the M5 to Durban. Jaco, Elmarie and little Junie Carter-Retief. A familie.

Jaco floors the accelerator and sets off towards Cape Town. The acceleration is pap. They also have sea down there but no bananas. He starts to sing. 'Ring Of Fire'. He doesn't know why. He can't explain it. Maybe this is what Elron Hubbard calls the free flow of energy. Something like that. Or maybe exteriorisation which is when you leave your body behind.

That's me. That's Jaco Retief. I left my body behind in Nelspruit. *I fell into a ring of fire. A ring of fire.*

21

Nellie has decided that we are going to be married in Cape Town. Lucinda wants to be the chief bridesmaid, and little Isaac will be a page. His status is still unclear, and we don't want to contemplate what might happen when he goes home. If he has a home. Now we can't imagine being separated from him. We see him as our child too. He is standing beside the pool, armbands in place, ready to dive. In he goes. He paddles furiously and climbs out so that he can dive again. We watch him as he waves a salutation. He gives the impression that he feels he must humour and console older people.

'I dived, Grandpa.'

'You did, Isaac. A lovely dive.'

'Yes, I did. I will do another one.'

'Okay. One more.'

In he goes, paddling like an insect when he surfaces. I move to lie on a sunbed next to Lucinda.

'Darling, we have to know about Isaac. Won't you tell me the whole story? We are anxious.'

'You don't need to worry, Daddy. His parents are both happy that he is here. I have emailed them a few times. No complaints.'

'Yes, but you are on a false passport.'

'Daddy, I had to bring him. My boyfriend, actually he's my ex-boyfriend, was doing a lot of drugs, he was mashed most of the time, and his ex, Isaac's mother, is also a complete disaster. She's even been an expensive hooker. I mean, that's no life for Isaac. I should know. I am clean now, although they say after you have been clean for two years, only then can you begin to talk about a cure. Thanks to you I had proper treatment.'

'Sure, sure. I can imagine that it's no life for him. But how does this all end, Luce?'

'It will be okay, Dad. I will look after him. I will get custody in the States.'

'I was hoping you were coming home to London.'

'I have some unfinished business in California. Then I'll come.'

'Will you still have Isaac?'

'I hope so. Do you want him to come to England?'

'Of course, if it's legal.'

'If I had a choice, I would stay right here. He loves it, I love it, but I must go back.'

She has always had an adamantine quality; I can't ask her why she has to go back.

There's a pause.

'Dad, it's fine. Honestly. Just trust me. And I will come to Sweden too. I love Nellie.'

'Okay, but please, please tell me if things go wrong.'

'I will, Dad. I've got the idea. Now for the wedding planning: I am looking forward to that. I'm like wildly excited in fact.'

Nellie and I have told our close friends that we are getting married, and Alec has decided to come immediately, because he can't stand another minute of country life in winter. A surprising number are coming. The Swedish relatives have been soothed by knowing we are going to have a Swedish blessing as well, on the island of Grinda in the Stockholm Archipelago. The Wärdshus has already been booked.

Nellie and Lucinda take charge. They have met the young Anglican vicar who is going to take the service. His name is Tim Fetch. In his spare time he is a champion sea kayaker. He appears to belong to the Church of the Great Outdoors, Lucinda says.

'He also wants some of your favourite poems to be read out. He thinks that would be nice. He's quite happy-clappy. You might have to close your eyes and hug everybody.'

'Fuck, wedding's off.'

'Grandpa, you sweared,' says Isaac.

'I swore. Yes.'

'You did swear, yes, Grandpa.'

'Sorry.'

Isaac does another of his dives.

'What's your favourite wedding poem, Daddy?'

'Shakespeare, 110. You recite it, Luce. You know it.'

'*Let me not to the marriage of true minds / Admit impediments …*'

As she starts to recite, her voice goes right through me; I feel as if I had never heard it before. She stands with the sea behind her.

'*… love is not love*
Which alters when it alteration finds,
Or bends with the remover to remove:
O no! It is an ever-fixed mark,
That looks on tempests, and is never shaken;
It is the star to every wandering bark,
Whose worth's unknown, although his height be taken.
Love's not Time's fool, though rosy lips and cheeks

Within his bending sickle's compass come;
Love alters not with his brief hours and weeks,
But bears it out even to the edge of doom.
If this be error and upon me prov'd,
I never writ, nor no man ever lov'd.'

Lucinda smiles as she finishes. I am stunned. Her voice is wonderfully and unexpectedly rich.

'It is so beautiful it makes me cry,' she says.

'Crying is a family weakness. You spoke it beautifully, darling. Perfect.'

'It is so beautiful. Will you explain some of the words to me?' Nellie asks.

'Of course, Nell.'

Nellie asks Lucinda the meaning of 'bark' and Lucinda tells her it means boat, as in 'embark'. I watch them together, Lucinda translating cheerfully. I ask Lucinda if she will read the poem at the wedding.

'Okay. I will. If you and Nellie really want me to.'

We do.

I drive out to the airport to get Alec. I see that one of the boxy little taxis has rolled off the road into a culvert. A police van is there and an ambulance arrives. Four feet poke out from underneath a grey blanket beside the road.

I drive cautiously to the airport. When he emerges from the sliding glass doors, it is immediately obvious to me that Alec is in poor shape. He sees me looking and tells me that he has had a minor stroke. He says it is only a transient ischaemic attack:

'That means it has gone, as the name suggests. I will live. But I am not allowed to drive for six months, which is a bugger. And I am not really supposed to fly either, but luckily I have friends in high places.'

The stroke was brought on when he found that his girlfriend, the Latvian lap dancer and budding anthropologist, had stolen a large sum of money from him before leaving for the Baltic forests. He asks me not to tell anybody.

'I don't want to look like a silly old fool. Which of course I am.'

'Have you been in touch with her?'

'No, I have not. What a stupid question. My lawyer has put the Latvian police on to her. But it's not really about the money, Frank, it's more about my naïveté in convincing myself that she liked me. It's horrible to think that all that sex was a ploy to steal my money.'

'Did she take a lot?'

'Five hundred grand.'

'Jesus, that is a lot. Still, you've got plenty.'

'As I said, it's not about the money. Listen, I envy you marrying someone like Nellie. There is something wholesome about her.'

'You always say that.'

'Yes I do, because I mean it.'

'That she is wholesome? Is that a compliment?'

'Absolutely, in my book it is, and by the way I am not convinced that you deserve her.'

'She doesn't do lap dancing.'

'Thank God for small mercies.'

He idealises Nellie because he can't really get on with women and their more complex feelings. So he has created his own image of

Nellie, the perfect woman, wholesome and fragrant. Upper-class Englishmen of a certain age are often awkward and dismissive of their wives. This may be a phenomenon that is passing, but Alec is beached, a right whale on the strand. I imagine his ex-girlfriend is even now planning to build her family a lovely home in the deep forest, impressing them all with her London sophistication. Despite his many millions and many wives and many girlfriends, Alec has never understood women because at a certain level he is frightened of them.

He is not staying with us because all beds are taken, but has booked himself into an expensive hotel looking across the Atlantic to Robben Island. He would like to come to the house later, perhaps for supper. He looks a little confused. I drop him off; he is walking more carefully than I remember, as if he isn't certain of where his feet will fall at any moment. But he is already instructing the porters and greeters vigorously as he heads for the lobby. I feel the urge to hug him, and he looks a little reluctant, but soon relents and I hold him close for a minute at least.

'You've always been a friend, Alec.'

'I love you, Frank. Before you get nervous, I love you in a manly way.'

I drive back along the coast road. I take note of the sea conditions and the wind and the mountain, with its blankets of cloud pouring over the flat table like dry ice before evaporating. I stop to watch seals – the active branch of the seal colony – driving an unseen shoal of fish into a small bay. The sardines have arrived. The seals are corralling them, working like sheepdogs. Now they have the fish trapped; they dart about, diving and leaping at high speed, to keep the fish in a compact group. They emerge from the depths, swallowing and leaping, bright silver fish in their mouths. Their indolent colleagues at the harbour should see this and learn.

When I am living here beneath the mountain and close to the sea, I feel alive. I have read that mountains were revered in prehistory because they were believed to be the gathering point of all sacred knowledge. And this mountain above us, always in view, always changing with the wind and cloud, has a similar effect on me. It is probably no different from the consolation believers who live near huge cathedrals, like Rouen or Ely, enjoy; it was the same urgent need to be fixed in the universe that caused palaeolithic man to assemble rock cairns and standing stones in Cornwall.

Osip Mandelstam wrote, 'I have cultivated in myself a sixth sense, an Ararat sense: the sense of attraction to a mountain.'

Me too.

When I am comfortably tucked up in Notting Hill, I dream of this mountain and its attendant, and often unruly, sea. I also marvel at the small daily natural dramas all around, like the seals rounding up fish.

The preparations for the wedding have been under way all day. Nellie and Lucinda are firmly in charge of the arrangements. There will be twenty-five people at the lunch. There will be simple posies of local flowers for the bridesmaids and something more elaborate for Nellie. The vicar, Tim Fetch, says that some of his customers – his word – opt for a bower of roses in the garden. If he's honest, he thinks it is just a little kitsch. He is wearing pink-and-black Lycra cycling shorts. He has come by bicycle for the consultation.

Later Nellie and I walk on the beach, each of us holding one of little Isaac's hands and swinging him with every second stride. He says, 'More, more.' Bertil waves from the life-savers' hut, where he is now a regular. We wave in return, and we feel honoured. Isaac deserts us and runs, in his own unstable fashion, along the sand towards the young lovers. They don't seem to mind his presence. They promise to bring Isaac home for the barbecue. As we look back he is chattering away.

The last surfers are far out there on huge waves. They bob like corks on the mountains of water, disappearing from sight for long seconds as they wait for the ideal wave. Behind them the cormorants are heading home to roost, flying in anxious, determined formations. They overnight on a huge block of flat stone, almost as big as an aircraft carrier, which can only have fallen from the mountain into the sea many thousands of years ago.

'It frightens me just to see these kids out there,' says Nellie.

'Me too. Even when I was young I was often frightened.'

'Is that the point? To conquer your fear?'

'Partly. Also to have friends. But it is the simple fact that this is something that doesn't demand money or dictate what you do or how you do it. In my day, free spirits were called "soul surfers".'

'Were you a soul surfer, Frank?'

'I tried. But it was a little too precious for the local boys.'

On the way up the path through the bushes we kiss. The air is fragrant. We are free in our own way.

'My soul surfer,' she says, still amused.

Alec arrives just after I have lit the fire. He has commandeered a huge car and a driver.

'Good God, something is on fire,' he says.

I tell him that it is a form of heresy to cook indoors when the weather is good. The wind is quickly dying as the sun sets and the smoke is rising straight up in a regular column, like the smoke from fires in Cowboy and Indian movies.

Alec is gazing down towards the beach.

'Beautiful. You are a jammy sort of fellow, aren't you, Frankie? Bum firmly in the butter.'

Alec's slang is about thirty years out of date, but strangely endearing. He is wearing a panama.

As she brings the plates and the salads and makes sure everyone has a drink, I feel guilty about Lindiwe. She looks happy, as though this is her life's work. Less than eight miles away, her husband was clubbed to death with a Coca-Cola bottle. Her own young children live in rural nullity with her mother. I have given Lindiwe money, which has enabled her to build a house in her mother's village. I have paid for schoolbooks and clothes. I adore Lindiwe, yet our relationship is fatally unbalanced: she depends completely on my good will and maybe, I sometimes think, she is obliged to pretend to be fond of me. At the same time I want her affection; it is important to me. At times I think that we are very close, but I know that in reality we are separated by our different lives.

Now, in this smoke-scented, gentle hubbub, I see Lucinda handing around grilled oysters on Melba toast – a Lindiwe special – and in the very familiarity of it I find hope: the hope that Lucinda is with us for ever, free from the hell she has been through. This evening she is so beautiful, so composed and gentle and warm, that I am convinced she is, as she said, over it. Now I induct Alec into the ritual of the *braai*, sacred in these parts. Lucinda appears and puts an arm gently around my waist. The children have gathered and some neighbours have arrived; one of them, Neil Battersby, was at school with me years ago. Neil is spattered with sunspots now, so that he has a snow-leopard appearance. He wants to lend his unique skills to the barbecuing. He believes you should never start cooking until the embers are white. He also recommends damping the fire with beer from a can when it is too fierce. His wife, Eleanor, raises her eyebrows eloquently. Alec is staring at the fire as if mesmerised. He moves off cautiously, to talk to Nellie who is talking to Marlene Cook, the wife of Barry. When she discovers that Nellie is Swedish, Marlene says she longs to go to Sweden. She wants to see the Northern Lights and deep, deep snow. She thinks her northern European ancestors are calling to her, reminding her of who she is. It's a race memory. Or a phyletic memory, the memory we don't even know we have. It's nonsense, but it is one of the theories that distract South Africans from looking too closely at what's around them.

Still, I think Marlene would find a trip in the Arctic north rewarding, even fascinating. A few years ago Nellie and I flew to Kiruna, inside the Arctic Circle, where the plane landed on skis, and we travelled onwards by dog sled to the Ice Hotel. We were wrapped in reindeer-skin rugs. The huskies were heart-breakingly eager. It was our first escape together from London and toxic memories. We both felt a little jittery, as if we were impostors. The sun, which barely rose above the horizon, produced an unstable and magical half-light that suggested the twilight of the gods. For miles the huskies bounded along, yelping in their ecstasy. It was impossible to resist the feeling that we had arrived in a mystical and myth-laden landscape.

The Ice Globe Theatre, a replica of Shakespeare's Globe on the South Bank, made entirely of ice, stood on the bank of the frozen

Torne River. The next night we watched a performance of *Hamlet* in Sami. Hamlet entered on a sledge drawn by reindeer. We sat on reindeer skins, in temperatures of minus 30 degrees Celsius. It was one of those moments you know you will never forget: as we left the Ice Globe, the Northern Lights descended from the heavens and performed their mysterious, swirling rites.

Little Isaac is once again stealing the limelight. He is enchanting. He asks 'How are you?' of everyone. Lindiwe is still trying to teach him to speak Xhosa, as if that is his inalienable heritage, and he can now say a few words, for instance, '*yebo*', yes, and '*molo*', hello. He said goodnight to me yesterday, '*Ulani kahle*' – and '*Molo*, Grandpa', good morning. I adore his eager, questing conversation. And I am happy because I know that I am free at last of my foreboding about Lucinda, which has never left me for a single day in five years. Every day I would wake up calm and be struck immediately with the knowledge that my daughter was a junkie. She is reassuring me now by putting her arm around me. She squeezes my waist: 'Are we getting just a little chubby, Daddy?'

'Have you been talking to Nellie?'

'Yours to guess and mine to know.'

She slips away to help Lindiwe. Not too far out to sea a huge tanker passes very slowly; its lights are blazing and twinkling so that it looks as if an exotic travelling circus has arrived.

22

I have ditch the car a week maybe five days ago. I let it run over a cliff near Graaff-Reinet where there is plenty of clapped-out cars lying in the bottom of a *kloof.* I was hiding for a few days. Now I am riding in a *bakkie.* The owner of the *bakkie* is a farmer in the Karoo. He says, *Jy stink vreeslik.* You smell awful. Fuck him. He won't say that if he knows I have a Beretta in my pants.

After a couple of hours I tell him, *my ou maat,* I need to piss.

Me too, says he.

Here's a good place for a slash.

We stop by a picnic table behind some big rocks in the middle of fuck all. It can be the Hex River Pass, I don't know. While he is pissing I get out my gun. He starts squealing when he sees the gun.

Don't shoot me, please. I have children. Please.

I can shoot him and push him over the black-and-white stones what stops you driving off the road and into the bushes below, nobody is going to find him there never except maybe a hungry leopard. I tell him thanks for the ride now give me the keys. He's so frightened he's wet himself and he's already had a piss.

Don't go crying to the police. Just say someone stole your car while you was taking a leak. Unnerstan?

Yes thank you. *Dankie.*

The *bakkie* goes quite fast. Three hours to Cape Town more or less. It's a Volkswagen. VW is always good engineered. First class, *bakgat*. I can see the wine lands now down there maybe near Wellington where Piet Retief was born. He should of stayed at home.

I am thinking what if Wynand is not dead and what if Elfrieda has gone to the cops and little Junie, how's she. 'Ring Of Fire'. It cheers me up but I can't think right. I want to talk to Oom Frank. He's clever. He's *slim*. He can make a plan for sure. But I don't know where my *oom* lives in Cape Town. I can't ask nobody in case the cops comes after me. Then I have an idea maybe he is in the telephone book. Cape Town/Kaapstad. I ask a lady who has a café place at the top of the pass with fruit and sweets and biltong and dried sausage and magazines if she have the Cape Town phone book.

Are you all right? she says.

Tannie, it looks like I may have maybe killed someone who is fucking my wife but I am okay.

I don't say this. I say, no fine, Tannie, thanks, and you?

No not bad can't complain.

She gives me the phone book. There's a hell of a lot of people in Cape Town.

In Potch the phone book only have about thirty pages. Can you believe it – F. D. J. McAllister, with address and phone number, is right there. Menemsha, 2 Beachfront Road. What is Menemsha? Maybe it's Xhosa. I must get a map of Cape Town by the petrol station. Now I can see Table Mountain. *Tafelberg*. It does looks like a table. It's very windy outside. There's a sign to Strandfontein Beach and I go there and park the *bakkie* far away and then I have a dip because I am stinking for real. Shit, the water is cold. I duck my head under and it aches. I am the only person taking a dip. I dry myself extra quick with some paper. Two people is kite surfing. It's beautiful when they fly over the waves very high. Maybe I can fly also. My underpants is black so that's okay nobody can know it's not a cozzie. Near Cape Town I see a sign *We buy any car any condition no questions*. It's a place where they smash up cars for spares for sure. Chop it I tell them they gives me three thousand rand no receipt. These coloured guys talks very fast. For sure they knows the VW have been stolen and the sooner they chop it the better for everyone. It's big business all over the country. The police knows what's going on but they get money for going blind.

I walk into town past the docks. At the station I take a taxi-bus to Camps Bay. I buy a hamburger at Steers. Some of the chicks working there looks at me funny like I crawled out from under a rock. For sure I must get some new clothes. My beard is growing quick. It is black like my famous relative Piet Retief's beard. Some people says he had a touch of the tar. I don't know where to go. I must sleep on the mountain that is full with snakes. There's people living up there smoking *tik*. They chase me away. I walk along the sea road to find Oom Frank's house. Menemsha. It's dark. I walk on the beach near some very big rocks. There's a cave and I go inside to lie down.

23

The wedding is enchanted. It is at Babylonstoeren – Tower of Babylon – a wine farm out of town. Nellie and I had lunch there and she said wouldn't it be the perfect place for a wedding. For whom? I asked. For anybody, she said, smiling. Her smile is like the sun rising over the sea.

I think that one of the purposes of a wedding is to endorse the deeper human values that we rarely talk about. And yet there is always something mysterious, and a little unsettling, about weddings – unspoken doubt among the reams of overstatement: all those failed promises and all those disappointments to come.

Tim the vicar decided to bicycle out here; to him thirty miles is a walk in the park, as he put it. For him the cycling is undoubtedly the main event.

We have booked cottages for all the guests; as they walk from their front doors they merge to form the procession heading in the direction of the parterre at the back of the main house. This parterre is to act as an outdoor cathedral. Tim the vicar is relaxed about our divorces. God, in his opinion, loves us all equally. Nellie and I follow behind Tim who has changed out of his cycling shorts and is wearing a cassock. The parterre is a kind of Garden of Eden, a bee-loud glade. We were assailed by the scent of rosemary and roses and thyme and allium. Guinea fowl screech, bees hum, ring-necked turtle doves burble. It's a low-level symphony.

Nellie is on Bertil's arm; she wears a cream dress, and carries a posy of little bell-shaped lily of the valley, peonies, white and pink roses, lavender and cornflowers. I am wearing an ivory suit, with a yellow rose in the buttonhole. I am escorted by Alec. Lucinda has a shorter version of Nellie's dress, and carries a smaller posy. She and Isaac walk together, each with a yellow rose as a buttonhole. Isaac is dressed in long velvet shorts in a kind of burgundy colour and a floppy antique white shirt, which Lucinda found in a market in Cape Town. In his long shorts, Isaac is dignified, regal, a young Haile Selassie. He appears to know that this is an important occasion and he also appears to understand what is required of him. He carries a present for Nellie, which he can't wait to open. This present has acquired a sort of symbolic importance, although no one has said what it is. Lindiwe carries a posy too; she wears a dress that she and Nellie chose. Alec is my best man; I have some worries about his medical condition. He is wearing his panama with the band of colours of the Garrick Club around the crown. He says he is fine but I think that another stroke is possible. He has the ring firmly under his control, although he is a little unsteady on his pins, as he puts it. The bridesmaids, including Lindiwe, follow behind us.

For the service, Nellie has chosen a sort of bower under a huge indigenous tree. We have opted for the 1662 version of the Book of Common Prayer:

Dearly beloved, we are gathered together here in the sight of God, and in the face of this Congregation, to join together this man and this woman in holy Matrimony; which is an honourable estate, instituted of

God in the time of man's innocency, signifying unto us the mystical
union that is betwixt Christ and his Church; which holy estate Christ
adorned and beautified with his presence ...

The words are enduring and powerful. They are too grand for
the marriage we have in mind. I wonder just what 'man's innocency' might have been. And I also think of Emma Woodhouse
writing of the selfsame wedding service 'the part in which N takes
M for her wedded husband, for better for worse'. Nobody now
takes the 'for worse' option too seriously.

When we are safely married – rings exchanged, vows made, red
roses handed over, kisses and hugs, prompted by Tim the vicar,
complete – Lucinda reads her sonnet. She is standing under the
dense tree, which is inhabited by small, busy green birds. I think
they may be white-eyes. These birds provide a light and cheerful
accompaniment, a squeaking encouragement to Lucinda's reading.

'... *love is not love*
Which alters when it alteration finds,
Or bends with the remover to remove:
O no! It is an ever-fixed mark,
That looks on tempests, and is never shaken;
It is the star to every wandering bark,
Whose worth's unknown, although his height be taken ...'

Lucinda's assured recitation and the words she is speaking are
profoundly moving for all of us and for many different reasons.
Nellie looks at me from beneath her little jaunty hat of blue silk.
kiss her.

'I proclaim you husband and wife.'

Our friends clap and whistle.

We move to a courtyard where the lunch is spread out on long tables under a vine. Geese fly, screaming their anxiety above the round hill, which stands inexplicably all on its own – as if in a previous age it was a tumulus.

My best man stands up to speak; he says that not just the women of the New Forest but women all across England are going to be upset when they hear I have married. Then he asks the guests to explain, if they can, how I managed to bewitch such a beautiful and serene woman. There are cries of 'Hear, hear!' and more whistling, led by Lucinda; her two-fingers-in-the-mouth whistle is piercing; she mastered it at a very young age.

Both Nellie and I speak. She says that I am a wonderful man, kind, generous and surprisingly knowledgeable. She says that she is astonishingly happy to be married to me. 'Frank has changed my life for ever,' she says finally. She kisses me and presses herself to me for a few long moments. Her body is conveying its own complicit message to me.

'Let her go, you beast,' Alec shouts.

He may even mean it. There's a kind of desperation about him, so different from how he was in his pomp when he had the arrogance and the almost visible self-esteem of an emperor of finance.

It's my turn:

'To our friends and family gathered, I want just to say how wonderful it is to see you here, in this beautiful place. My life, too, has changed out of all recognition since I first met Nellie. She has brought joy into our lives, and I have been incredibly happy and lucky. To marry her is to have squared the circle. Please drink to Nellie and the life to come.'

We toast Nellie and the life to come.

'But I also want to say a word or two about Bertil, this upstanding young surfer and apprentice heart-breaker, who has been astonishingly tolerant and charming. Bertil, I want to thank you; I know that I am not your father and that I am not going to replace him in any way, but I just want to tell you, so that there is no misunderstanding, that the closer I come to you, the happier I will be. To Bertil.'

Now Bertil stands up.

'I want to say that I am like totally happy that my mom and Frank have gotten married. My mom is so happy and that has made me happy. She deserves happiness, believe me. And Frank, I want to thank you for everything. Frank, this place is like totally awesome, bru.'

I give him a knuckle bump to cement our burgeoning relationship.

'A moment, please,' I say. 'I have one more thank-you. Lucinda, I want to tell you that having you here with us has been an utter blessing. I have always loved you, as you know, and these few weeks together have reminded me, if I needed reminding, just how much I love you. Immoderately is the answer. We also adore little Isaac, but that is a story for another time. To my beloved daughter, Lucinda, thank you for reciting so beautifully, and being so innately beautiful yourself. And thank you to Nellie, my wife.'

Nellie hugs me, and Lucinda joins in, sobbing, and Isaac comes to lend succour, his hair more like a nimbus than ever.

The afternoon slows. There is a heavy calm all around. The calls of the turtle doves in the oaks have become subdued. Some of the party take to their cottages to swim or to sleep. The swimming pool is deliberately styled on the traditional round cement farm dams that I remember so clearly: here a deck is raised up all around the dam, with loungers and piles of pristine white towels and tables of wine and juice. A woman, with a little *kappie* on her head and swathed in a deep green apron, comes around carrying a tray of brightly coloured fruit lollies, home-made. Guinea fowl are taking a dust bath. A tortoise staggers along a path, driven by some prehistoric and half-understood urge.

Nellie, Bertil, Isaac and I walk the length of the astonishing parterre, through walls of espaliered pears and across lawns of thyme and camomile and under trellises of many fruits and vines heavy with red and white grapes. Water is being directed through channels towards the various parts of the garden, each one a small fiefdom. I see, as if it was yesterday, the tongues of water setting off to feed the dry soil of Welgelegen. I can't fully understand why it affects me so deeply; without warning, the water in the channels has produced a Proustian moment: I see my childhood and my patchy history and my Tannie Marie and my beautiful mother.

We walk on towards the small hill, the ziggurat that gave the place its name – Tower of Babylon.

'Frank, are you all right?' Nellie says.

'Why do you ask?'

'You are looking a bit, I don't know, worried for a moment. Preoccupied.'

'I was thinking of my childhood when I was left with my aunt, Tannie Marie, on the farm miles from home. We have come a long

211

way. My aunt used to read to me from *Pinocchio* by candlelight; I am sure I told you all this. It's never left me. It all came back to me, how baffled I was, and how I didn't understand the reasons why I was dumped there and I remembered my father telling me my mother had died. You probably think I am crazy, but these channels of water running into the garden remind me as if I were there. Nellie, darling, I love you. Never leave me.'

'I love you, Frank. *Med hela mitt hjärta.* With all my heart. I will never leave you, darling. Thank you for what you said about Bertil. It was so powerful.'

'In a nice way?'

'Yes, it was perfect and so generous. And what you said about Lucinda was wonderful too. You made her cry.'

'We Boers have a tender side. We cry easily.'

'Yes, I have noticed.'

Little Isaac and Bertil are crossing a stream and heading towards the hill. Neither of us broaches the question of Isaac's future. Anyway it will depend on Lucinda.

We set off up the Tower of Babylon from the relative cool of the garden to the baking sun of the climb. The way up is strewn with smooth brown rocks, which contain iron. Two stones knocked together give off a metallic sound. From the top of the hill we see endless vineyards, the old Cape Dutch house and outbuildings and in the distance rows of mountains, baking in the sun, gently out of focus behind a blue haze.

Before dinner we have music to dance to. It is *langarm*, which means long arm. Under lanterns in the trees, five local musicians play the accordion, a banjo, a trumpet, a saxophone and drums.

212

We all dance; we have been seized by madness under the rising moon. I have the first dance with Nellie, each of us at arm's length, the traditional *langarm*. Then I dance with Lucinda. Vanessa and Bertil dance. Vanessa's parents dance. It's strangely liberating and carefree and reminds me of my roots. My school friend, Neil, and his Eleanor know all the moves. Neil manoeuvres Eleanor vigorously, as though he is drawing water from a rural hand pump. Nellie says it's like country dancing in Sweden.

Finally, exhausted, we swim and get ready for dinner. Lamps have been lit to mark the way to the cottages and to the main house. We are in a febrile state. There is too much emotion in the air, too much expectation, too much energy, too many hopes. The moon has now risen directly above the strange, symmetrical, lonely hill. This southern moon is the colour of aged Cheddar and so close that I can see its valleys and mountains.

I feel that we have been born again, that we have shed our too-tight old skins, like puff adders.

24

The name Menemsha is cut into some wood and painted gold. I am waiting. There is nobody at home. I am most of the day staying in the bush by the end of the beach and sometimes I walk a long way to the harbour by a beach where moffies stands naked, *kaalgat*, not any clothes on except a hat. Their cocks hangs out. They don't care. They fuck in the bushes white and black it's all the same. When I am walking yesterday they was whistling me. If one of them comes near me true's God I will kill him. I have some money still and I buy two pies at Pick 'n Pay and a jack of brandy. I eat one pie now and keep the other for the night. I like the chicken pie and the steak the best. There is boats unloading by the harbour. Maybe I can get a job on a boat and go to some place like Namibia so nobody will find me. Now I walk back along the beach. It's still hot. The *mofgats* seems to be gone. When I get to the house I see the gate is unlocked. I walk in. Down below I can see the swimming bath and the *outjie* who is cleaning it. He's a coloured guy holding a long pole. There's lots of them around here. The first coloureds was born nine months after the Hollanders landed. This *outjie* tells me I cannot come in.

Listen, I am the cousin of Mr Frank McAllister. *Hy* is my *oom*.

They are not here.

Where are they?

Mnr Frank and his lady, they got married somewhere.

Married? When they coming back?

It can be tomorrow.

Just give me the code for the garden gate.

I am not allowed to do that, sorry. I am not allowed.

I take out the gun:

Now you are allowed. Give me the code. I am here to check the security for my uncle but if you wants to make trouble I can shoot you. You unnerstan?

Ja, sorry, *meneer*, I unnerstan.

When are you coming back here?

I work here once a week, Thursday, sir.

Okay, just stay away while I check out the security. Security is my business and my uncle have asked me to do it. He have sayed he will be home this week. So you give me the code and then you fuck off for a week. You unnerstan?

Yes, *meneer*, I unnerstan.

I tell him: you must test the lock for me to see.

Okay, *meneer*.

You sure you unnerstan?

Yes, sir.

He test the lock for me and he give me the code.

Goodbye. If you know what's good for you, you won't come back until next week.

I walk around the garden past the swimming bath and the *braai* area. The doors of the house is locked. The swimming bath has a little wooden house by there. It has cups and glasses and water inside there. This shall be much better than sleeping in the bushes or with all those *bergie* coloureds. They are high on *tik*. They don't even know what they are saying. They all talk *kak*. Their teeth has fallen out. The cupboard in the store-room is full of mattresses and cushions and so on. All sorts. Even Nescafé and powder milk. Bum in the butter like my uncle. He will help me for sure. He knows the big shots, they can make a plan. I'm sitting in a lounger, that's what they call it. They have a lot of loungers in Sun City where I met that girl with the big tits, Casey. I wish my girls was here with me they would love it here. Maybe Oom Frank will lend the place to us for a holiday. I am eating the steak pie. And drinking some brandy. I feel great. 'Ring Of Fire'. June and Johnny. What a song. I am falling asleep happy now, chilled.

25

We are driving home after three days. Alec had to go early for a check-up in Cape Town. The wedding has had an adverse effect on him. He says he feels even more isolated and lonely as though it has become difficult for others to see him. As though he is a fading fresco, he says. He tells me he has given us a painting as a wedding gift; it can be collected from Sotheby's whenever we are home. He won't tell us whose work it is. It's a surprise, he says.

We see a sign to a crocodile farm and turn off. The reality is not so much a farm as a series of pens with cement pools, a gulag, containing hundreds of crocodiles, many of them destined to be shoes. You are not supposed to loathe whole species, but it is difficult to like crocodiles. They are designed entirely to kill. Every so often something alarms the crocodiles and there is an awful chaotic scramble for the water. I remember my school friend who was taken by a crocodile; I can't imagine a worse way of dying.

Also, Nellie says that we should go: 'This is really horrible, Frank.'

'We're out of here. I am so sorry.'

Isaac says, 'Goodbye, crocs.'

As we drive down the corrugated dirt road, I ask Nellie if she thinks I have been insensitive.

'How could you know what it would be like, Frank?'

I had assumed there would be a few crocodiles taking their ease in bluish, natural and clean ponds – very different from the frightful, nightmarish, mêlée which took place below us in the filthy water. I am glad that Lucinda went ahead with Vanessa and Bertil and Vanessa's parents.

As we come down the pass we see Table Mountain in the distance.

As always, I feel myself subject to the attraction of mountains: *We read landscapes, we interpret their forms, in the light of our own experience and memory, and that of our shared cultural memory.*

We are all pleased to be going home. Our mountain, our sea, our house, all are waiting. We have another two weeks before we go back to England. Bertil can't wait to surf with Vanessa, and Lucinda has an appointment to go to see the Hand Spring Puppet Company in Cape Town. She would love to learn how to make giant puppets. Maybe she could get an internship there. Putting behind me memories of her false starts, I encourage her. Sometime soon we have to discuss Isaac's future with her. The strange thing is that Isaac has dropped into the world from nowhere: he appears to have no memory of his mother or father, and never mentions his home. But he is only two years and a few months old, if Lucinda is giving us the true facts.

We decide to have tuna grilled on the fire tonight. Lindiwe wants to help but I tell her to rest. She seems to be disappointed, so I ask her to make one of her potato salads and Nellie will make her famous mayonnaise. Lindiwe dons her housecoat.

I arrange the wood and light the fire. Bertil has gone off with Vanessa and now he calls to ask if Vanessa can come for supper. Of course, if her mom doesn't mind.

I understand. As a boy I was susceptible to the superior attraction of my friends' houses and even of their parents. When my mother died, the house died with her. Disloyally I thought that our house was dreary by comparison with others'. So I am pleased that Vanessa wants to come to Menemsha. I have seen that there is something about Nellie that children find very attractive. They understand immediately that she is always interested in them and does not have to feign interest, as so many adults do. Like Georgina, who saw Lucinda only as a prop in her glamorous social life of buying hotels and losing money. God, what a weight has been lifted from my shoulders.

26

I hear the car coming and the gate opening to the underground parking. I stay in the pool house because I don't want to just *sommer* say hello, here I am, Oom, in your pool house. I must phone him and say I want to talk to him serious – can I come over to see you sort of thing. Maybe we can have a beer. I must get up early tomorrow to phone from the harbour before anyone shall find me. Now I see Oom Frank and them around a *braai*, the fire is burning in the *braai* place on the other side of the pool. Two or three of them is sitting in chairs. The maid is walking with a tray from the house. I can hear them laughing and speaking. They's happy, no worries. Maybe they has had a drink. Oom Frank says loud okay let's *braai*. Soon I can smell the fish cooking. I don't like fish, only fish and chips. I like *Snoekies* by the harbour. They knows how to make it – the best. Fresh fresh fresh. *Vars vars vars*. I don't know if Oom Frank will help me again. I juss don't know. But all these important people has friends who can make things right. I mean he gave the Scientology *outjies* $50k, that's a fuck of a lot of money. No skin off his nose.

It's dark and the fire is nearly dead. The lady says okay I am going to bed I am tired, forgive me. What for? I don't know. Oom Frank says I will be up soon, darling. This should be his new wife. And my wife and Wynand who can maybe be dead, how are they?

I have dropped them right in the shit. I must get away where I can take Junie and Elmarie and Elfrieda. But maybe she doesn't want to speak with me no more. If Wynand have not attacked me we can be in Durban with the Banana Boys right now eating ice cream and seeing the snakes, black mambas and so on, in the snake park. They has had shark nets for years there, no trouble. Now they are trying nets at Fish Hoek. I was a *doos* telling them at Cape FM to shoot sharks but it was because I was drunk. Everyone knows I was totally pissed – totally wrecked like they says in California. Maybe I can go back there one day.

I am falling asleep on a stripy lounger.

I need to take a piss. I look out of the window. Now they is all in bed or in the *sitkamer*. I go round the back of the pool house and take a piss. I see the light is still on in the sitting room. I can see someone standing up and another person gets up. A boy and a girl, it looks like, goes out through by the gate. I lie down on the stripy mattress again. I must get up early in the morning.

27

Only Lucinda and I are awake. We are waiting for Bertil to come back after walking Vanessa home. We are listening to music and talking. She has her head on my shoulder. It seems to my susceptible mind that she is happy to be close to me.

'Where do you think the lovebirds are?' I ask.

'Lovebirds? Don't be an old fogy. But snogging on the beach would be my guess. Don't panic, Dad.'

'I want to go to bed.'

'I will wait up for them. I am quite happy here.'

I kiss her.

'Thanks. That's kind. Goodnight, darling. Don't forget to put the alarm on when Bertil comes in.'

'I won't. It was such a lovely wedding, Dad. And you made a great speech.'

'Thanks, my darling.'

I pop into Isaac's room to see if he is all right. He has a small room of his own now. He is sleeping, clutching his teddy bear. For a moment his hands are opening and clenching. There is something magical about a child's bedroom. Isaac's hair spreads out on the pillow, framing his face, so that he has some of the aspects of an icon. I can't let him go.

As I slide into bed, Nellie, half asleep, whispers, 'Hello, darling, it's so good to see you again. My husband. I love to say that.'

Her breath is warm and enticing. I want to tell her to look at the moon on the water; it is like pewter, gleaming rather than shining. But I don't suggest it because I know I am too ready to push people to admire a view or the birds or the protea bushes or even – as the other day – little tongues of water advancing across the parched earth. Georgina's diagnosis is that I am an insecure colonial, always too ready to make a point: *It's not English, Frank. Believe me it really isn't.* Even now I can hear the contempt in her voice.

The pleasure of curling up with Nellie, my wife, is intense. I kiss her and she smiles, half asleep. We don't speak; we don't need words at this moment, as if we have made a fair exchange of our essences.

I wake up. The light is still on in the big house. The creepy-crawly starts up. There was a green snake in the pool yesterday. I hit it with the pool scoop. I hate snakes. I can't sleep no more because I must get up in a few hours. I have a dop of Commando and I eat half the meat pie what's left. I go outside the pool house for a piss by the flowers. There's a helluva lot of flowers and bushes in this garden. The moon is shining on the sea. Oom Frank has got every fucking thing he wants even the moon shining up his arse. We have fuck all. What that *outjie* says in the Oliver fucking Tambo Airport is right: *Ons is nou die kaffers*. We are the kaffers now. But we are the real South Africans the real Boers and we lost everything what is belonging to us. Stolën. We made this country and we have been verneuked, cheated. I must drink some more brandy. Not too much because I have to stand up early. Fuck, there is someone in the garden. It's two o'clock. I hide in the pool house and look out the window. Now there's another munt just behind. I cock the Beretta. Ten up. Two black guys, kaffers, is walking slowly around. They go to the maid's room. I see them taking her to the house.

I wake. There is a terrific noise somewhere in the house. It's a chaotic, terrifying sound, of shouting and breaking. Now Nellie wakes up.

'What is it, Frank?'

'Don't move. I will go down. Just don't move. I'm calling security.'

The phone is dead. I hit the button by the bed which sets off the alarm, but that is dead too. I run to the sitting room. Lindiwe is tied up and two men are fastening Lucinda's wrists behind her with cable ties. She is sobbing gently.

The men turn to me. 'Good evening,' I say.

You must engage them. I remember someone saying that: *You must speak to them.* I am not frightened; a torrent of anger is drowning out all fear. I would kill them if I could. There is a presumption and an entitlement to these people here in my house that incenses me. I walk towards them.

'Stay still.'

One man holds up a machete and makes a chopping gesture to suggest what could happen to me. The second man produces a gun.

'We must talk,' I say. 'You can take what you want. The car, money, credit cards, anything, I will show you. But please don't hurt anybody.'

'If you lie to me I kill you,' he says.

I know that in many robberies the intruders choose to kill the witnesses because the police make so few arrests. Survivors can cause trouble. There is even a belief that some robbers take revenge by raping any women present.

I can't see them clearly in the gloom. It is the gloom in which horrors traditionally take place, as if there are particles in the air presaging something frightful.

'You must give to us every-ting: money, keys, credit cards with pin code and your car. If you do that you can live.'

I detect a Congolese accent.

'*Vous êtes congolais?*' I say. '*Du DRC?*'

'*Vous parlez français?*'

'*Mais oui. Bien sûr. J'étais quelquefois a Kinshasa. Je peux vous aider.*'

He hits me on the side of my head with his hand. It's a warning. He thinks I am up to something. He smells of liquor. The other man points his gun at me. Still I am not afraid.

'This is my daughter. She has a child. I will give you whatever you want, but you must leave my daughter and the others. If you want to take me in the car to get the money that is okay.'

'Take your clothe off,' the man with the gun says to Lucinda.

The second man is not happy about this proposal. He shouts at his colleague, waving his hand towards the door. He turns to me:

'You get everything you 'ave, like you 'ave said. Bring it all here in this room. No cell phone. This man come wif you. Or we kill your daughter and you also.'

226

I lead the man with the machete all around the house. I tell him that my wife is in bed. *Au lit*, I say. We enter. Be calm. Nellie asks if I have Isaac. I don't. The man with the machete waves at Nellie – go out. I tell Nellie that she must go to the sitting room.

'Try to stay calm, darling. I will handle this.'

She is wearing my dressing gown.

I give the man our cell phones and wallets and all the credit cards. I go with him to my study where I open the safe and take out the money. There is about two thousand pounds. Then I write down the pin numbers on a piece of paper. We have four credit and debit cards. I take off my watch and give it to him. I give him our two iPads and a laptop. I am stumbling through a nightmare.

My phone and the laptop are traceable.

'*Je peux vous aider,*' I say.

'*Comment tu fais ça?*'

'*On peut faire un plan. Je peux retirer beaucoup plus d'argent de ma banque en Angleterre. Mais ça dépend d'une chose, si vous êtes d'accord. Ma famille doit être libérée d'abord.*'

In fact it is impossible for me to get cash from my bank in the middle of the night but I am hoping to keep him interested after they have taken everything, so that they don't kill us.

We come back into the living room and place the phones and laptops and money and watch on a table. As the first man inspects what we have brought, I see Isaac coming down the steps, holding his teddy bear to his face.

Isaac says, 'Hello, Grandpa.'

The gunman turns, startled. He fires at Isaac but misses. Nellie runs towards Isaac.

'Hello, Grandma,' he says, as Nellie grabs him, her back to the gunman.

They are going to kill both of them. I move towards the man with the gun.

Now I hear a voice, screaming. There is another man in the room: he has a dense black beard: '*Ek is Retief*. I am Retief,' he shouts. 'You people are dead.'

Oh God, it is Jaco. He fires at least five shots, hitting both of the men in quick succession as they turn towards him. The noise of automatic gunfire in close proximity is appalling – a staccato promise of death, each deadly shot producing the same, lethal, report. Jaco shoots the two men again as they lie bleeding. One of the men is bubbling audibly from a wound in his throat. Jaco kicks him in the face – two teeth hang from his broken mouth. Jaco is in a frenzy. To my inexpert eyes the intruders look as though they are already dead. There is a terrible amount of blood, not just on the floor or the sofas but also on the walls.

Now Bertil comes to the front door. 'I heard gunshots,' he says. Nellie rushes to him. But Bertil may have had a few drinks; it takes him a while to understand what has happened. I ask him to go back to Vanessa's parents' house and to call the security and the police from there. He goes off.

'Jaco, thank God for you. You came just in time,' I say.

'No, only a pleasure, Oom.'

I have no idea what he is doing here. I am shaking and disoriented. In my confusion I think Jaco must have appointed himself our guardian angel. He is still holding his gun.

'*Ja*, I am sorry, Oom, I have been sleeping in your pool house for a few days while you was away.'

I hug my cousin for the first and last time. I have to sit down. My legs have become loose, like a puppet's, like Pinocchio's.

Isaac is serene. Perhaps he thinks we have been playing a game. But the rest of us – apart from Jaco – are trembling, shocked and horrified. Only Jaco is inured to the horror; he is drunk and elated. My legs won't respond. I want to be sick. I throw up into a waste-paper basket. Lucinda is sitting, still tied, her eyes fixed lifelessly on the near distance. She is silent now. Lindiwe has freed herself and comes to help me struggle to my feet. I get some scissors from the kitchen and cut Lucinda's cable ties. Lucinda is silent. I think that she will always blame me in some way for this cataclysm, this horror. But she says under her breath, 'I'm all right, Daddy.'

Nellie and I hug her as if to bring her back to life; Isaac, not wanting to be left out, joins in. All around us there are bloody fragments of bone and even a small section of hair and skin flung onto a sofa; the floor where the two men lie in a grotesque intimacy is awash with blood. A mohair Swazi carpet is soaked. Who knew that a human being harboured so much blood?

Even in this appalling nightmare, Lindiwe tries to help Lucinda. She brings water and three Lemon Cream biscuits, and Lucinda eats them all as though she is hypnotised.

'Don't cry,' Isaac says. 'Can I have a Lemon Cream?'

Contained within Isaac's innocent concern is a message: it is that I will never see my beloved country again.

GRINDA

Four months later

We set out from Stockholm into the Archipelago on a fine summer's day. The ferry pushes away from the quay in front of the Royal Dramatic Theatre, where Greta Garbo studied. I love the view of the city receding and my spirits are instantly lifted by the cheerful, determined way the ferry strikes out for the island of Grinda. This beautiful Friday afternoon the whole of Stockholm seems to have taken to their boats and headed for the distant islands of the Archipelago.

It's a beautiful sight. But we are subdued. I see that our happiness has been fatally undermined. But Nellie has never uttered one word of reproach. She believes fervently that *love is not love/ Which alters when it alteration finds*. The Swedish relatives are arriving tomorrow for the blessing of our marriage. A happy occasion.

After what happened to us, I think that we are incubating something like a bacillus, something repulsive and untreatable. I see that, like my eager ancestor with his dreams of Eden, I had a naïve faith in my sense of being protected by my special understanding. I have spent many nights awake. In those waking hours I see my house drenched in blood, the walls spattered. The nights have become difficult for me. I have often had to move from our bed to a sofa or a spare bed. I must endure my personal torment and my regrets alone.

Thank God for Jaco, our Caliban, who turned out to be our saviour. Who knows what would have happened if he hadn't appeared? In fact I can guess all too readily.

I have bought the family farm in Potchefstroom and put it in trust for Jaco. The trustees have evicted the cousins. Jaco's children and his wife have moved onto the farm, to live in the old house where Tannie Marie used to read *Pinocchio* to me by candlelight. Jaco says he has given up drinking. His firearm licence has been revoked, however. Wynand survived being shot, and did not press charges, partly because I gave him some money to go away. He also had a few misdemeanours on his own record. For one, he was already married. Jaco says the children love the farm. They run around barefoot as often as possible, in the traditional fashion. Jaco is planning to buy Nguni cattle. They are tough.

Nellie has hired the Grinda Wärdshus, which once belonged to the first director of the Nobel Prize. He bought the whole island and built the Wärdshus in 1906 as his holiday house. Nellie likes the idea of people coming from all directions by ferry. It strikes a seafaring note. It was here on Grinda that I was entranced by the celebration of Sankta Lucia. Lucia is also the name of our Lucinda; it means illumination. In mythology Lucinda is the giver of first light.

Our Lucinda went back to California to see her ex-lover and to return little Isaac to his mother. We would have loved to have him live with us; it was heart-rending to say goodbye. He was calm, hugging us, saying goodbye, and at the same time giving the

231

impression that he was ready for the next adventure. Lucinda insisted that he had to go back. She promised to bring him to see us if his mother agreed. To be honest, she said, his mother would be delighted to get rid of him. She wants to be in the game, although Lucinda didn't tell us what game that might be. I hope it is just a figure of speech.

Bertil is with us. He is still in touch with Vanessa, and he has been talking of going to Cape Town to see her, against his mother's wishes. In four months he has grown and he has become very handsome. I see girls looking at him. I have a surprise for him: I have paid for Vanessa to come to the Wärdshus. She is already there.

The boat stops briefly at Vaxholm – once the home of King Gustav Vasa – before we head out again. The flotillas of small and large boats are surging out to the islands, many under sail. I have the feeling that the Vikings would have had a similar sense of infinite possibility as they sailed and rowed out to the open sea on their daring and improbable voyages. The sea girdles and cossets the myriad islands and skerries, some so small that they are host to just one or two trees and a clapboard house – usually red – with a dinghy moored out front; others are bigger, clothed with fields and forests and blueberries. The eider ducks paddling inquisitively in busy flocks and the reeds in the shallows suggest that the Baltic is not very saline here.

Nellie says she knows all the best places to swim on Grinda. They have been imprinted by her childhood memories. We will swim together. Perhaps she sees the immersion as being something like a baptism or a washing away of sins.

★

Vanessa is waiting at the dock as planned: a blonde, slender beach girl. Poor Bertil is startled when he sees her. They are too young to handle this level of emotion in public; Bertil kisses her perfunctorily. He looks at Nellie and me, expecting an explanation.

'It was your mother's idea,' I say.

'In fact it was Frank's idea but I think it was a good one. Sorry, darling, if we gave you a shock.'

Bertil soon gets over his discomfort. Vanessa takes his hand. Our luggage is ferried to the Wärdshus on a trolley. Vanessa and Bertil walk off hand in hand along a path that opens onto a meadow of wild flowers. The last time we were here I saw that the Swedes have an almost pagan regard for nature. Rocks and tumuli and groves of birch engage them. A small house near the jetty, which doubles as an art gallery, offers paintings of the island and detailed studies of wild flowers and a few pictures of Hydra in the Aegean Sea.

Once we have settled in, Nellie leads me to a beach she remembers. First, it is obligatory to pick up Grinda Loaf at the store, she says. We scramble down through some trees to get to the beach and we swim in the warm, brackish water. Nellie's swimming style reminds me again of my mother's; it is graceful and measured. We lie in the early summer sun on the crescent beach eating Grinda Loaf. We are the only two people there. It is an enchanting place. It breathes good will and reason. Eider ducks swim by. They have a neat and bourgeois appearance, mildly quacking once in a while. Nellie says she wants to buy a cottage out here. But in my fickle heart I wonder if it wouldn't be just a little boring. Perhaps I could learn to sail a boat or practise ice fishing in the winter. On the way back to the hotel we buy an ice cream, the best ice cream in the world, Nellie says. I tell her that no one forgets the ice cream they had in their childhood. I tell her about the Green Parakeet Café in Fish Hoek, which sold only three flavours of ice cream.

'Was it lovely?'

'No. It was a dump. But it had a green parrot in a cage. I tried to speak to it.'

'Successfully?'

'No, it bit my nose.'

More and more often I think of my childhood. After the appalling bloodshed in my house, I am constantly reassessing my life as though I might have been responsible for what happened. As though I were wilfully courting disaster in some way. As though being a careless Retief may have been a factor in what happened.

We four dine together in the Wärdshus. We feel privileged to have Vanessa and Bertil with us. As you get older you need to be in proximity to young people, to fortify yourself with their youth. There is nothing more dispiriting than older people who have sunk below the horizon, from where they utter their muffled discontent.

Soon after noon the next day, the guests start arriving, and Nellie introduces me to her friends and relations. I imagine them looking me up and down, assessing, in their polite, intense Nordic fashion, if I am good enough for their home-grown Nellie. I imagine that they know what happened to us. I feel clammy and unwelcome and in some sense diminished. The men hardly speak at first, while the women go into huddles and exchange information about babies and divorces and children. After a few drinks the men become vocal. They have a chortling, communal laugh, uttered unexpectedly.

The blessing is given by a Lutheran priest; it is short and to the point, wishing us happiness and godliness. Why not? Both are desirable. And I need help. There are toasts in aquavit. Nellie's two brothers and a cousin speak, saying what an exceptional sister and cousin she has been. The men make a roaring sound: *whoar, whoar, whoar* – expressing their approval without recognisable words. Then we move to another room where a huge smorgasbord of gravadlax and herring and Arctic char and cinnamon cakes spreads into the distance. The scents of cinnamon and dill float around us solicitously. Some of the friends and family are soon very drunk. I am drunk. I am actively seeking oblivion. We dance and we sing and we go to bed late. Lucinda sends us a text message, asking for photographs, and she says that little Isaac is fine and that she has already made progress in adopting him. His mother has died of an overdose.

There are aquavit headaches at breakfast: saunas and swimming are the favoured antidotes. On my way for a swim I see children gathering wild strawberries and stringing them on lengths of grass. It is the most innocent activity I have ever seen. In its simplicity there lurks a reproach for me. I think of Lucinda and her troubles; she hardly had a childhood and to add to the charge sheet I have, with my familial lack of judgement, subjected her to unimaginable hell. I start to sob, and head for some trees and shelter. She says she has adopted little Isaac. They will be coming in September.

We make our way back to Stockholm in the course of the following day. At the airport an email pings onto my phone: Alec has died of a catastrophic stroke. I can't tell Nellie; I don't want to upset her at this moment; she is staying on for five days in

Stockholm with her family; Bertil and Vanessa are staying with her to see the sights. I need to be home, not for any obvious reason but because I feel that I should be home with my books and my paintings and my house where I will calm down and where, alone, I will possibly be able to shake off the fear that I am responsible for what happened.

Jaco is probably a psychopath. He suggested when I last saw him in Potchefstroom before going home that he had upheld the honour of the Retief family by killing the two Congolese. He sees himself as the victor of this particular Blood River. His view is that it was them or us. This is, of course, a natural law.

When I have unpacked I set out for Sotheby's to pick up the wedding-present picture – now also a legacy – given to us by dear old Alec. I walk all the way from Kensington Gardens and on through the park, which is in full bloom; I see that the early daffodils have died off, so giving a rural effect to a gently billowing hillock in the grass; and in the famous flowerbeds, and climbing upwards on ropes and trellises, roses are heavy in promiscuous flower. Swans are landing heavily on the Serpentine as though it is their first ever attempt at this difficult manoeuvre. Egyptian geese are investigating potential nesting sites. Horses pass listlessly on the bridleway. They are chivvied into a canter and the sound of their hooves – perhaps I am imagining this – makes the earth resonate deep down. There are no Romanian gypsies to be seen.

I walk through Mayfair, past the casinos and oligarchs' town houses and long-established restaurants and beautiful churches and unexpected small gardens.

Sotheby's has delegated a tall slender Italian woman to lead me to my picture. She tells me her name is Ilaria. With long, delicate fingers – her nails a deep dark blue, almost exactly the blue of my Parker's school ink – she unwraps the brown paper to reveal the painting.

'I love this painting,' she says. 'It is so beautiful, so special.'

It's a Howard Hodgkin. A banker friend of mine has a Hodgkin above his desk in his office and I have always admired it, as Alec knew. The banker, Julian Tubal, told me that his cleaner had reproached him for buying a painting by someone who is so hopeless that he paints all over the frame.

Ilaria is waiting for me to say something. I am silenced and disconcerted as I look at the painting.

'I 'ave been tol-e-d that your friend 'as died, I am so sorry,' Ilaria says, briefly placing her elegant hand to rest on my arm. 'You will remember him by this picture I am sure.'

I accept her kindness gratefully. I need it at this moment. Ilaria is right: I will remember ridiculous, pompous, kind and generous Alec.

'Yes,' I say, 'I will remember him. He gave me a job when I was young.'

'Very special friend, for sure,' she says, with her gaze directed to the picture.

She wears a lot of black and blue make-up around her eyes, giving her a Nefertiti appearance.

Now she wraps up the picture expertly. It's a special talent to be able to wrap unruly parcels, one I don't have. She hands me the parcel. I thank her. I want to embrace her. She strides away elegantly in her black dress, and turns back to me with one warm glance. I want to speak to her about the deeper meanings of art, but she has gone.

Also, I wanted to tell Ilaria that the deep red tide of my Howard Hodgkin, escaping over the frame of the picture, will remind me for ever of venous blood – dark red, depleted of oxygen. I am an expert on this subject. It has infiltrated my dreams for the last few months. It has entered my being. And I know that I will never be able to put behind me the memory of the torrents of blood that desecrated my beautiful house. Dark blood has been projected and fired right to the top of the walls to make awful congealed patterns. And the blood formed puddles and meres and eddies that overflowed out into the landscape in trickles to become rills and streams that in turn became rivers. Further down the hill, the blood was finally reclaimed by the dry soil, leaving, for a while, only a damp trace, which faded fast.

I saw that I had come full circle.

Acknowledgements

I would like first to acknowledge the wonderful James Gill, my agent. Without him I would be adrift.

Publishing is a complicated, many-facetted, enterprise. Over the years with Bloomsbury I have come, more or less, to understand what everyone is doing. And these are the people who have worked patiently and calmly on my books.

Michael Fishwick is my editor and plays a key role, one of reassurance and light discipline. And lunch. Anna Simpson has been diligent and cheery and kept the process moving smoothly. Thanks too to Madeleine Feeny and Anika Ebrahim. All the people who sell the books in to bookshops are, as I have seen at first hand, both indispensable and persistent. I have seen Bloomsbury's sales team in action, and they aren't easily fobbed off.

I would also like also to thank Alexandra Pringle, Kathleen Farrar, Richard Charkin and Nigel Newton.

Writers, inhabiting their own, self-serving world, are not necessarily the best choice of partner, and I acknowledge warmly all that my wife, Penny, has done over the last many years.

A Note on the Type

The text of this book is set in Bembo, which was first used in 1495 by the Venetian printer Aldus Manutius for Cardinal Bembo's *De Aetna*. The original types were cut for Manutius by Francesco Griffo. Bembo was one of the types used by Claude Garamond (1480–1561) as a model for his Romain de l'Université, and so it was a forerunner of what became the standard European type for the following two centuries. Its modern form follows the original types and was designed for Monotype in 1929.